THE LIST OF
Last Chances

Caitlin Press Inc.
3375 Ponderosa Way
Qualicum Beach, BC V9K 2J8
www.caitlin-press.com

Text design by Derek von Essen
Cover design by Sarah Corsie
Edited by John Gould
Printed in Canada

Caitlin Press Inc. acknowledges financial support from the Government of
Canada and the Canada Council for the Arts, and the Province of British
Columbia through the British Columbia Arts Council and the Book Publisher's
Tax Credit.

Library and Archives Canada Cataloguing in Publication
The list of last chances : a novel / by Christina Myers.
Myers, Christina, author.
Canadiana 20210099062 | ISBN 9781773860596 (softcover)
LCC PS8626.Y367 L57 2021 | DDC C813/.6—dc23

THE LIST OF
Last Chances

BY CHRISTINA MYERS

CAITLIN PRESS
2021

For my mom, who always said that I could.

1

THE KEY CLICKED in the lock a split second before the shouting began.

"Ruthie! Hey, Ruthie, get up. You have to look at this."

Jules slammed the door behind her and dropped her keys on the table, the metal hitting the glass with a bang. I squeezed my eyes shut tighter.

"Ruthie. Jesus, are you still asleep?"

I was under the blanket, head and all, but I knew she was looming over me. Waiting. Vague disapproval in her voice and presumably on her face. I groaned. "Jules, just … no."

I had no energy to respond further. My mouth was dry, my head pounded, and my back hurt from having slept on Jules's lumpy old couch for so many weeks in a row. Somewhere on the floor next to me was an empty bottle of wine; I wasn't sure if I'd left the wine glass there too. Actually, I couldn't recall if I'd even used a wine glass. I groaned again.

"I'm not going away this time," she said. She wasn't joking; there was a newly enthusiastic level of determination in her voice. "I'm going to stand here till you sit up. I have something important to show you."

I held out another thirty seconds, but after she cleared her throat several times at increasingly loud volumes, I gave in and pulled the blanket down. I had to squint against the light coming in through the window across the room. The sky was blue, puffs of cloud rolling on a slow breeze. I imagined it smelled like the ocean, the way a perfect late summer afternoon always does on Prince Edward Island: warm and soothing but with the crisp scent of autumn around the corner.

I didn't actually know how it smelled. I was relying on memory to imagine such a thing. I hadn't left Jules's apartment in at least a week. Maybe ten days.

"I found a job for you," Jules said, jamming a piece of paper into my field of vision, blocking out the blue sky and clouds. "I found *the* job for you. This is *your* job. It's perfect. It's *exactly* what you need."

I struggled to keep from rolling my eyes at her. I'd spent the last six months hearing all about what I "needed" from well-meaning co-workers, a parade of friends, my boss (former boss, now, but he'd done his best to keep me employed as long as he could) and my family—at least when I answered their calls. No one knew what I needed. I didn't even know what I needed, for God's sake.

"Okay, thanks. That's great. I really appreciate it. I'll check it out," I said, nodding a vague thanks in her direction.

But I didn't think it was great, and I didn't appreciate it, and I already knew with utter certainty I definitely was not going to check it out.

Jules knew the same, of course. She pursed her lips and sat down on the far end of the couch, forcing me to pull my feet out of the way.

"I'm not leaving you alone until you read it. The whole thing. And then we're emailing the guy who posted it. I'll sit here all day smelling your funky wine-hangover breath until you do this. I'm not joking," she said. "By the way, you have caveman eyebrows. You need to get them waxed, like, three weeks ago."

She smiled and stared at me, waiting.

"Fine. Hand it over," I sulked. "And I don't care about my eyebrows. In case you hadn't noticed, I don't care about anything. At all."

Appeased, Jules smiled at last. "Find someone else's couch to have a midlife crisis on, then. But first, read this. It's perfect, Ruthie. It's just perfect."

She said "perfect" slowly, letting it roll off her tongue in a soft but dramatic way: purrrfect, the "T" at the end like a soft, gentle cap on the sweetest-sounding word of all time. She handed the paper to me, and I glared at it, my eyes still blurry.

> WANTED: Experienced care attendant to accompany elderly client by car from New Annan, PEI, to Vancouver, BC. Must have safe driving record and be comfortable driving a minivan. Successful applicant will assist client in packing up residence, then drive client to her family in Vancouver. Accommodation, food and other expenses for trip will be covered, as will return airfare/travel costs. Must be friendly and efficient and must provide good company and support for client prior to travel, during travel and overnight if required. References required; would prefer someone with five-plus years of experience providing in-home care assistance. Apply with resumé to David at d.march@tripp-engineering.com.

I read it a second time and then skimmed it once more. I bit my lip and noticed again how awful my mouth tasted. I wanted to lie back down on the couch and not think about this job that Jules had deemed was *purrrfect*. I couldn't make my way to the grocery store lately, let alone across the entire country. Jules stood, awaiting a verdict, and I tried to make a face that implied I was giving genuine consideration to the idea.

"I don't want to do this," I said at last, handing the paper back without looking at her.

"I know you don't want to. But you have to."

"No. I don't." I pushed the blankets the rest of the way off and stood up. The wine bottle clattered on the wood floor as my foot swiped against it. I was still wearing the jogging pants and T-shirt I'd put on yesterday. Correction: the day before yesterday. My whole body hurt. My head hurt. Most of all, my heart hurt, not in a poetic way but an actual physical ache through my chest. How could I do anything at all, even the simplest of daily tasks—never mind drive from one side of Canada to the other—when I wanted to just lie down and not get back up ever again?

"I'm not going to do it, Jules."

"But—"

"I'm not going to do it."

"But don't you think—" she started again.

"No, I don't," I barked back. "Jesus, just … leave me alone. Okay?"

I shouldered around her and headed toward the bathroom. "I'm going to take a shower."

"Good, you stink like my dad's fishboat," she said, unfazed. "I'll start working on your resumé."

I flipped her the finger, stomped across the small apartment to the bathroom without looking back to see if she'd noticed, and slammed the door behind me. There was no way I was going to apply for that job. Not today. Not ever.

＊

My bones ached as I stepped into the hot water. I felt eighty, not thirty-eight-and-counting: my back sore from sleeping on the couch, my eyes tired and puffy from what had become a daily ritual of drinking too early, staying up too late and sleeping past noon. My skin was hot and tight, a flush still running through me from drinking too much the night before—and all the nights before that, going back to February.

It was impossible not to think of *it* when I was in the shower, because I'd been in the shower that day too. I'd just shut the water off and started wrapping my hair in a towel when I heard the faintest noise in my apartment: the clicking of the door opening and then a second click when it was shut. *Jack's come home early*, I'd thought to myself, and then, when I heard low noises: *And he's turned the TV on.*

I'd smiled, adjusting the plan in my head as I quietly towelled off. It was perfect, really. I had come home early myself, part of a little plot I'd come up with to celebrate Valentine's Day. Jack had always hated Valentine's, refusing to go out for dinner or even to a movie, complaining of the long lines and busy crowds on "forced consumerism day." So I'd gone shopping for his favourites (steak and asparagus and mashed potatoes), and I'd come home early to surprise him—I'd be all dressed up, hair done, meal cooked when he got home from work. But now it seemed that he, perhaps, had conjured up the same plan. I'd have to skip the "all dressed up, hair done, meal cooked" part, but that was okay. This might be even more fun. I tiptoed to the bathroom door, turned the knob as slowly and quietly as I could manage, and let the towel drop to the floor. I'm not terribly brave about my naked body in general, but that day I'd thought, *What the hell, it's Valentine's*, and I threw the door open, stepped out, fanning my arms like a showgirl, wiggled my rear end and shimmied to make my breasts bounce—an intentionally semi-comic, semi-sexy manoeuvre.

And there was Jack, on the couch, half-naked himself, flopping about like a convulsing octopus. Complete with extra arms and legs. And the sounds I'd thought were the TV—that I'd imagined were the low chatter of voices on *Law & Order* or *Maury*—were actually moans and giggles. Girly moans and girly giggles. And then it was silent—total, hear-a-pin-drop, not-a-single-sound silent—as two sets of eyes swivelled up at me.

All I could say was: "Fuck. Me."

Fuck, yes. Me, not so much. Jack was midway through shagging the clerk who worked in the flower shop under our apartment.

✴

I stepped out of the bathroom with a towel wrapped around my body and a second one on my hair. Jules was at the kitchen table with her laptop open.

"Let me see the job posting again," I said, without looking at her.

She grinned, and I swear I saw her bounce in the seat as she handed it to me. I avoided looking at her, instead scowling at the paper and grabbing it with more force than required.

She'd folded up my blankets and tidied the couch cushions; the wine bottle was nowhere to be seen, and the sliding door to the balcony was open to let some fresh air in. I could feel the tickle of the breeze over my damp skin, and I shivered as I sat on one end of the couch to reread the job description.

"Where did you get this?" I asked.

"It was on the bulletin board at work."

Jules and I both worked for Just Like Family, a seniors' home-care agency that placed care attendants with clients all across the island who needed help in their homes. Well, technically, Jules worked for Just Like Family. I *had* worked there for more than nine years, but I'd phoned in sick so many times in the last six months that my boss finally let me go. Gilbert had looked sad and shamefaced but determined; he'd probably hoped that the shock of being fired (and the sudden loss of income that would come with it) might jolt me out of my funk. It hadn't worked.

"Gilbert told me about it," Jules continued. "He said, and I quote, 'I just got this interesting request; it's on the board. No one has seen it yet, so no one will realize if you take it down. For Ruthie.' So I went and looked, and I put it in my purse."

It made my throat feel tight to hear it. Poor Gilbert, still trying to fix things for me. I could imagine his face as he'd said this to

Jules: *For Ruthie.* Probably with a sad, tired look in his eyes, like a big brother who was worried and disappointed all at the same time.

I scanned the description again. It was hard to argue that it was, as Jules had claimed, perfect. Food and accommodation paid for; several weeks of travel, which would take me away from PEI and Jack (and Jules's couch, though she hadn't yet suggested she minded my presence); and, presumably, a decent paycheque at the end to boost my pennies-away-from-empty savings account.

"I don't know," I said to Jules.

She made an exasperated sound and rolled her eyes. "You don't know what? That you need a job? That you need to get away, maybe, and try something new? That you need to have more to do in a day than watch *Judge Judy* and drink another bottle of wine?"

She closed her eyes and took a deep breath. "Ruthie, something *has* to change. You can't just go on like this forever. Shit happened, it sucked, you've cried, and it's not fair, and it's not easy, but come on already. You're forty. Are you going to spend the rest of your life moping around about the fact that Jack-ass Jack-off Jack did you a favour by letting you know what an asshole he is?"

I didn't know what to say. She was right. About almost everything. "I'm not forty," I said. "I'm thirty-eight."

She just stared at me, one eyebrow raised, expectant, and waited for me to say more.

"Jules," I sighed. "Look, the thing is, I've worked at the same place for, like, a decade. I don't even know where my resumé is, and anyway, it's so outdated by now I'd have to start from scratch. That will take ages. This guy needs someone right now. And I look like hell; I have nothing to wear. I can't do an interview like this. And … and also, I was thinking of maybe going to visit my parents soon."

I threw in the last point on a whim, but it sounded good coming out of my mouth, as though maybe I had a plan beyond cocooning in this apartment forever.

"You can visit them when you get back. It's not a six-year journey through the Himalayas, for Pete's sake. And we'll find you something to wear for the interview. As for your resumé—ta-da!"

She turned her laptop toward me so I could see the screen, and from my vantage point on the couch, I could make out the rough template of a resumé. She held up a manila folder.

"Gilbert still had your old resumé in your file, along with records of all your clients. He gave me the whole thing. I'm already halfway through writing the new one."

She grinned at me, pleased with herself, and turned back to the keyboard. I tried to hold on to the scowl on my face, and my brain scrambled for another few good excuses to avoid the entire thing, but I smiled a little in spite of myself and stepped closer. Jules's enthusiasm on my behalf was hard to resist. I was lucky to still have her. I had basically invited myself to live in her apartment for months, and she'd never once complained, except to point out when I'd really gone past my shower expiry date. She listened when I ranted. And more times than I cared to remember, she'd come out on tiptoe in the middle of the night to check on me, pulled up the blankets, and let her hand rest on my shoulder while I feigned sleep, refusing to let myself cry in front of her.

I swallowed, nervous. "He probably won't hire me," I said.

"We'll see," she replied.

"I've never driven that far," I added.

"You don't have to do it without stopping. It's just one day at a time."

"I don't even have a suitcase," I continued.

"You can borrow mine."

"I hate you sometimes," I said, trying not to laugh but failing.

"No, you don't," she said. "You love me and always will. Now, get some clothes on and we'll finish this resumé. I have to be at Mr. Johnson's by 7:00 p.m. for his medication, and I want this resumé emailed before I go."

I opened my mouth to debate it, to tell her *no*, we could send it another time, tomorrow, next week, next year, never. But I stopped myself, watched her type and flip through my employment file, a small smile on her face. I took a deep breath and stood up to do what she said: get dressed. *Start with that*, I thought to myself, *just that*.

✳

At 6:35 p.m., I hit "send" on an email addressed to d.march@tripp-engineering.com, which had my resumé, a cover letter and a list of references attached. I listened to the computer make the *whoosh* sound of an email heading off into cyberspace and felt a wave of anxiety over my body, like a hot-cold flush rolling over my skin.

I didn't want this job. I desperately wanted this job. I didn't care if my resumé wasn't good enough. I prayed that my resumé would shine. I didn't want to leave the island. I wanted to get so far away that I couldn't remember what had happened here.

Jules grabbed her purse, readying for her appointment with Mr. Johnson and his blood pressure medication, and hugged me on her way to the door. "It's too perfect not to work. It's meant to be," she said, winking at me as she disappeared down the apartment hallway.

Maybe, I thought to myself. Jules was a fan of woo-woo things, reading her horoscope in the weekend paper for insight into her future. Next to her bed was a stack of books "based on real events" about alien abductions and ghosts, or biographies of famous psychics. She often claimed she had a "feeling" about things: if her teeth ached, it was a sign of something bad on the way; if she saw a black cat, it was a good omen. The last time she'd seen a black cat, she'd announced that something good was coming for me. I argued that *she* had seen the cat; therefore, if it meant anything at all, it surely was for her own good fortune, not mine—and anyway, weren't black cats supposed to be bad luck? But she insisted: something wonderful was going to happen.

Right about now, I'd have settled for enough money to pay all my bills—wonderful could wait.

I picked up the remote to turn on the TV, but before I could hit the power button, my phone gave a *bing*. I cast my eyes at it, assuming junk mail; all my old co-workers and friends had long since stopped inviting me anywhere.

It was a reply to my email and resumé.

"Jeez. Didn't take long to decide you didn't want me," I said under my breath, clicking on the notification.

> Dear Ms. MacInnes, thank you so much for your message. I've just taken a look at your resumé and background, and I was hoping I could have a chance to talk to you, so that if we seem to be a good fit, I can start calling your references tomorrow. I wonder if you are available right now? I realize it is short notice, but I would like to move forward with the hiring process ASAP. Sincerely, David March.

Shit. Shit, shit, shit. I'd been counting on having a few days' grace to think about this entire thing, and that was assuming they'd even be interested. He wanted to talk right now? I scrambled for a way to get out of it; I could, I reasoned, just pretend I hadn't seen his reply. But that wouldn't look very efficient or professional of me.

I replied: Mr. March, thank you so much for your interest and speedy reply. Yes, I would love to talk to you. My phone number is on the top of my resumé; please feel free to call anytime this evening.

I hit "send." *Whoosh.*

A moment later, a bing and a reply: Ms. MacInnes, if possible, I would like to do a video interview, via Skype or FaceTime perhaps? Let me know which works best for you and where to contact. Regards, David.

Double and triple shit. A video interview? I looked down at my shirt—I wouldn't even wear this to the gym. And I hadn't done a thing with my hair aside from brushing out the knots while Jules worked on my resumé.

> Hi Mr. March, yes, I can do that. My roommate has FaceTime on her laptop, so I will include her contact information at the end of this email. Can we make it for 7:30 p.m.?

I glanced at the clock. That would give me a little more than a half-hour to prepare.

Bing.

His reply: Ms. MacInnes, 7:30 your time works for me. Please call me David. Talk to you soon.

✳

A half-hour later, I was minimally presentable: my dark brown hair was pulled back in a bun, and I'd put on a blouse of Jules's that was roomy enough to fit my bigger chest and shoulders, along with small diamond stud earrings (a Christmas gift from Jack-ass five years ago, which I had nearly chucked in the toilet several times over the last few months). I had Jules's laptop arranged at an angle so that the glare from outside wouldn't be too harsh but would still afford a prettier view than simply the back side of the kitchen. FaceTime was open and ready.

And then I waited. I thought about that black cat and sent up a prayer that its omen had been about this moment, even though I was pretty sure that prayer, in general, was as useless as black cats and good omens.

My heart was racing. I checked the time again. I shifted in my seat. And just like that, I realized: I wanted this job, more than I had wanted anything in a very long time.

2

W<small>HEN THE MUSICAL</small> jingle of the incoming FaceTime call rang out, I jumped in my seat, a shot of adrenaline sending tingles down my arms and legs. I had that roaring zoom in my head that usually occurs when I'm giving a speech at a wedding or I've tripped and fallen in front of strangers. Panic, mixed with fear, and tinged with embarrassment. The computer continued to trill away as I stared at the screen, frozen, until—realizing the call would hang up if I didn't do something—I hit "accept." The screen went from black to an out-of-focus blur of light and colour.

"Hello?" His voice boomed through the speakers, a deep, low sound with enough of a twinge of nerves in it to help ease my own just a little bit.

"Hi," I replied, my voice breaking like a frog croaking, as though I'd not spoken to anyone in months—which is sort of what it felt like, truth be told.

"Ms. MacInnes?"

"Yes, it's me," I replied.

He sounded confused, and I wondered if the hasty preparations had left me looking not so much "suitable employment material" and more "wayward bum."

"I can't see you," he said.

I looked at the screen. Everything was still a blur, like the Wi-Fi was having a hard time catching up.

"I can't really see you either," I said. "It's all just fuzzy."

"Oh, hold on."

The fuzzy blob that was Mr. March moved around, the camera panned up and down as though he was adjusting the lid of the laptop, and then suddenly the screen was filled with his face.

"Oh!" I said.

He wasn't necessarily good looking, not in a magazine-and-movie-star sort of way. If anything, he had a grumpy look about him, serious and intense, though this was softened by his unkempt appearance. His full beard and moustache had gone a week or two past a needed trim, and his dirty blonde hair had probably not been combed this morning. He was also young, much younger than I'd imagined—maybe just a few years older than me. Why had I assumed he was older? The tone of the job posting? The wording in his emails? He rubbed his hand over his hair, messing it further, and stared with confusion right at me.

"Oh," I said again, realizing too late that it was the second time I'd uttered it.

"Can you see me?" he asked. "I still can't see you; it's still black on this end."

"Is it?" I said, my eyes casting over the screen, trying to figure out the problem, my brain scrambling to catch up. Jules had plastered a piece of black electrical tape over the camera lens at the top of the screen. She'd put it there after she'd watched a creepy video on You-Tube about webcams being easy to hack, allowing random strangers to watch you any time your laptop was open. "Hold on, the camera's taped over; my roommate put it there. Just a sec, I'll pull it off."

So much for a smooth kickoff to the interview. I yanked the tape off, wondering if it had left a streak on the lens, and then looked back at the screen. I could see the tiny inset of my own face now, a small screen in the corner of his larger one.

He was absolutely still, no movement at all, staring at me. For a second, I wondered if the connection had been cut and the image was frozen. But then he shifted just slightly.

"Hi," he said.

"Hi," I replied.

"Hi," he said again.

It was like two people meeting in a doorway and both moving left and then right, at the same time, to let the other pass. Neither of us seemed capable of the next logical step.

"Hi," I said, feeling daft. "So, umm, thanks for, you know, considering my application. For the job. The umm … posting, you know?"

Under the table, I pinched my own leg. *Snap out of it, idiot.*

"No, I'm so glad you emailed," he answered. "I'm getting a bit desperate. None of the candidates I'd found till now have worked out, and time is running out."

My eyes widened at that. So my resumé hadn't been so spectacular after all—desperation had motivated the quick call. He seemed to realize what I was thinking and put his hand up.

"I don't mean … well, that is, your resumé is great. I would have called you first, if I'd gotten your email first. I just got a lot of others before you, and a few seemed like good options, but my mom … well, you'll see."

He chuckled a little at this. Just then, I heard Jules's key turning in the door. I held my arm up to the side, off the screen, with my palm flat like a traffic cop.

"So did you have some questions for me?" I ventured.

"Oh, yeah, yes, definitely."

As he asked the questions, and I answered with what seemed to be mostly intelligent responses, Jules slipped past on tiptoes, padding over the wood floor, avoiding the creaky spots. She'd clearly figured out what was going on by the nature of the questions, and she was beaming, giving me the thumbs-up in my peripheral vision.

She inched closer, as close as she could without being in the screen, so she could get a full look at my potential new boss. I could tell out of the corner of my eye that she definitely approved—

her grin was wide as could be, and she did a little boogie butt shaking on the spot.

I kept my eyes on the screen, nodding as Mr. March spoke, chiming in with answers to his questions, giving examples of challenging clients I'd had in the past, sharing anecdotes about how I'd dealt with medication resistance or recognizing early-stage dementia. As I spoke, he nodded and nodded, his eyebrows still hugging together in the middle, totally focused.

Finally, he asked the question I'd been dreading. "So, will you be able to leave for some period of time, with your current employment?"

"Well, Mr. March—"

"Seriously, just David is fine."

"Okay. David. I'm actually sort of in a bit of a lull between clients at the moment, so it's kind of perfect timing."

It wasn't technically a lie. I *was* between clients, but only because my agency had been forced to let me go, not because there was a lack of them to be had. And the "lull" was more like a six-month-plus hiatus from my whole life.

He smiled then, not the sort of necessary smile that your coffee barista gives you when they hand over your double non-fat no-whip macchiato, or the smile that the person for whom you've held the elevator door gives you when they slip past you, but a real smile. Huge, like his whole face was smiling, his scrunched-up eyebrows relaxed, his grey-silver eyes crinkled up, his lips opened. Full-on toothy grin.

"Great," he said. "That's, yeah, that's really great."

I stared at him, dumbfounded. Did that mean I'd gotten the job?

"Well, look, Ms. MacInnes, I think I'd really like to hire you. I'm just going to call some of the references tomorrow, and then—"

"Ruth—just Ruth is okay. Or Ruthie. Most people call me Ruthie." Why did I add that? It sounded so childish.

He grinned again. "Okay. So I'll call the references and then you can go over and meet my mom. She gets final say, of course, so no guarantees. But I think you're perfect for it. Perfect. Just perfect."

I could see Jules off to my side, doing mini-cheerleading jumps, no doubt pleased as punch that he had echoed her "perfect" conclusion. If she could have given herself a high-five, she would have right then. In fact, it very much looked as though she was doing an NFL end-zone touchdown dance.

"Thank you," I said, smiling back at David, ignoring Jules.

"Thank *you*," he replied, emphasizing the latter word.

"Oh, thanks. Thank you. I mean—" I broke off, laughing, realizing we were back to two people in a doorway.

"Ruth, I'll email you the information for my mom, but I'm hoping she'll be home tomorrow and you can go right away."

"Sure, yes! Tomorrow. Sounds great. Sounds perfect. Definitely. Perfect."

Perfect, again.

"My mother, she's a character. Well, you'll see. So I'll email tomorrow morning with the address and the time, and we'll go from there. I'd better get going; I've got one more appointment here at the office before I head home."

My eyes flipped to the clock—quarter after eight at night seemed a bit late for an appointment at what I assumed, based on his email, was an engineering firm. Then my brain caught up and I smiled.

"Oh, I forgot, you're in Vancouver. Time difference. It's past eight here already. But still sunny; it's been a nice day."

I hadn't even experienced the "nice day," what with being hungover on the couch for almost all of it.

"I can see," he said, pointing at the screen. "It looks beautiful. It rained here today."

I wanted to apologize for the rain for some irrational reason, or to tell him about the sun at the beach this time of year, when summer is at its peak, like it knows it will soon need to give way for autumn—as though telling him about it would be almost as good as him going himself.

"Well, thank you, Ruth, and we'll talk soon."

"Okay, sounds good, David. Great. Yes, great." I wasn't sure if I was meant to hit the disconnect button, so I just waited.

He stared out at me another few seconds, then said, "Okay, good night," and his screen went black.

I swivelled in the seat, to look at Jules.

"I think I just got the job," I said.

"I think you just got more than a job," she answered. "Mr. Scruffy Beard there was a hottie."

"Yeah? I didn't notice, I guess."

Jules just laughed. "Sure, whatever you say."

3

IT TOOK AGES to fall asleep. I told myself it was nerves about meeting David's mother in the morning, but if I was being honest, it was only partly nerves. The real problem was that it was the first time in weeks I'd gone to sleep without being partially or fully bombed on a bottle or two of wine.

I couldn't even recall falling asleep most nights lately. And when I woke up in the morning, I was always greeted with a series of clues as to how the night before had gone. Was I in pajamas or still dressed? Was I under a blanket with a pillow, or just sprawled on the couch? Were there plates of half-eaten food or just empty glasses?

Being stone-cold sober made the process of falling asleep painful. It was impossible not to think of being in bed with Jack, feeling the warmth of his body nearby. He'd always fallen asleep easily, quickly. It seemed almost superhuman: he'd lie down, roll on his side (away from me) and less than a minute later, I'd hear his soft snoring.

At first it had seemed sweet, like a little boy falling off to sleep after a hard day of play. I had interpreted it as a show of his character, his good-natured approach to the world, his ability to let go of slights and hurts and not sit and simmer about them. The opposite of me, it had seemed. If someone cut me off in traffic, I was still pissed off three hours later while I told him about it over dinner. Jack just let everything roll off of him. He'd shrug his shoulders, smile, say, "Oh well, c'est la vie," and it was done.

Sometimes I'd try talking to him to keep him awake. It felt like a good time to talk about shy, intimate things, that cozy bubble of warmth at bedtime with just a small bedside light on. It worked, sometimes, but he rarely had anything revelatory to tell me as I poked and pressed for his secrets. "What do you think about in the shower?" I'd ask. "What did you think when you first saw me?" "Where do you think we'll be in ten years?" "What's your favourite thing to do in bed?"

He'd answer with the simplest of responses and follow with his famous Jack shrug.

"What are you looking for, Ruthie?" he'd say with a tone that landed somewhere between amused and irritated. "I don't have any secrets. What you see is what you get, babe." And then he'd roll over, and a minute later the soft snuffle of his snore would be all that was left of the conversation.

But he did have secrets, after all, didn't he? I'd been right to poke and prod, to ask and wonder. There were huge parts of Jack I'd never known at all, despite my efforts.

By two in the morning, I'd tossed and turned for hours and hadn't gotten even close to sleep. I wanted to get up and have half a glass of wine. A full glass. Two glasses. Instead, I got up and went to the washroom.

Sitting on the toilet, I opened my phone, tapped the Facebook icon and scrolled. There he was. Jack. Jack-ass Jack. The guy I thought I'd be with for the rest of my life, whose profile photo now included him, his flower shop girlfriend and flower shop girlfriend's miniature dog.

She was cute—the girl, not the dog (though of course the dog was cute as hell too). Flower shop girl was cuter than me by about ten years, blonde, and seemingly possessed with that supernatural ability some girls have to do their hair and makeup without looking like they're dressed up for a Halloween party.

What a bitch.

I refused to think about the fact that every time I'd ever interacted with her—and I had, many times, what with her owning the shop below our apartment—she'd been lovely. Not a fakey sort of sweet, but a genuine sweet. I'd once gone in to buy flowers for my client's birthday and left wishing that I was friends with the flower shop woman.

They'd both duped me, hadn't they? Jack with his "what you see is what you get," and Flower Shop Girlfriend with her kind (but obviously evil) demeanor.

As I scrolled through their photos from a recent trip to Cancun or Puerto Vallarta or some other amazing magical place that Jack had never taken me to, I waited for the familiar rage to rise up. In fact, I welcomed it. I wanted it to build up, boil over, fill me with its anger and self-righteousness. It was a thing to hold on to, to roll around in my brain, to bite and chew on, to distract me from every other pressing and current worry. But it wasn't there this time. Maybe it didn't have enough wine-fuel to get going. Instead of the familiar comfort of rage, I just felt so tired and sad that I wanted to weep, a thing I'd rarely permitted myself to indulge in.

I finished in the bathroom, padded back to the couch in the dark living room, crawled under the blankets, set the phone on the coffee table and let myself feel this new, strange sadness that didn't have any rage at its borders. It got bigger and bigger and bigger, until I *did* start to weep, the kind of bawling that sounds like a howling, wretched animal. I cried so hard that I started to gasp for air, big gulps between wails, pressing my hands to my face.

I felt Jules next to me before I heard her, and I rolled away, my face turning in toward the back cushions of the couch, horrified and ashamed of myself but still so relieved she was there. She kneeled on the floor next to the couch, put her hand to the top of my head and let her fingers slide down over my hair, the way my mom used to do when I was sick as a child.

"Shh, shh, shh," she said, over and over.

I tried so hard to stop crying, but her comforting only doubled it. How can something so small be so loving and reassuring? Why is it harder yet also better to have your grief witnessed, as if that makes it real and legitimate?

"I'm so sorry," I sobbed out. "I'm sorry, I'm sorry, I'm so sorry, I'm so sorry. I'm sorry."

"Shh. I know. It's okay, it's okay. It's okay, Ruthie, it'll be okay," Jules replied.

She said it over and over and over, a hundred times, a thousand times, and somewhere along the way, in between one "shh" and another "it'll be okay," I finally fell asleep, too exhausted to even dream or wonder where Jack was or why I hadn't been good enough to love, properly and forever.

※

David's email with instructions, as promised, was sitting in my inbox when I woke up. I lay tangled in my blankets as I read his message.

I was to be at his mother's home at 11:00 a.m., assuming that still suited my schedule. He included her phone number in case I got lost, but he warned that it was a landline, not a mobile, so if she were out in the yard or in the laundry room, she would not answer.

His message continued: I have advised her that you will be there, and she is to ask you whatever questions she may have. She can be very stubborn. And a lot of fun. I think you'll get along well. Please let me know after you've been there. Thank you again. David.

It was already past eight, and the drive there was about forty-five minutes, so that left me two hours to shower, get rid of the "cried all night" raccoon eyes, make something to eat and get going.

I pulled myself up to sitting and looked at the phone in my hand. It occurred to me, not for the first time, that I should remove Jack from my friends list on Facebook. My finger hovered over the icon on the screen to open it.

"Later," I thought to myself.

In the bathroom, I pulled my hair out of its bun, stripped out of my old T-shirt and stood in front of the mirror.

"Okay," I said quietly. "Here we go. You are going to get this job. You are going to be awesome. You are going to kick ass."

It was the sort of stuff that should have had a lot of enthusiasm and fire behind it. It had none. My voice was still hoarse from crying overnight, and my head was pounding—equal parts cry hangover, lack of sleep and, I realized with a start, the absence of wine the night before. The booze gave me a hangover, but now I'd gotten so accustomed to having it that *not* having it was apparently going to make me feel just as bad the next day.

"Fantastic," I whispered to myself, as I squeezed toothpaste out onto my toothbrush.

I critiqued my face as I brushed, zeroing in on the dark circles, the puffiness around my eyes, the zit that had somehow erupted overnight. Double fantastic.

I finished with the toothpaste and got the shower started. When it was hot, I stepped in. I wanted the water pouring over my head to feel symbolic, to tell myself it was a new day, that it was time to stop and let go and move on, that today was the first day of the rest of my life, or some other equally ridiculous and cliché claptrap. I wanted to feel that way, as I washed my hair; I wanted to believe that I was rinsing off the crap from yesterday and all the last six months—the last six years, for that matter.

But I didn't. I was still me. But I *was* awake. I was standing. I was on my way to a job interview. And most important, most strange, most unexpected of all: I wanted this job.

This was new. This was good. This, alone, was enough change for one week, I decided. I wasn't me, fully, again, but something had shifted, and that was good enough to start, I decided, as the water poured over my face and shoulders and disappeared down the drain at my feet. Good enough was something, wasn't it?

✳

I knew exactly where the house was. In fact, I'd driven past this property a thousand times on my way to Mr. Dooley's, which was only another mile or so up the road. He'd had a stroke, and his wife couldn't help him with all the things he needed each day, so for six months I'd come morning and night to lend a hand. He'd recovered so well—stubborn old bastard, as his wife had said—that eventually he didn't need my help, or even his wife's, and so my job there had been done.

It was a gorgeous bit of the island. Rolling green hills, with brown-red dirt lanes running between farm fields, old white clapboard churches with tall spires off in the distance. The sort of views that ended up in the calendars and art postcards that were sold to the tourists who streamed onto the island all summer long.

I pulled my car off the main highway and onto a long gravel lane, pausing just long enough to make sure that the address on the post sign at the juncture matched what David had told me. Ahead, a long driveway, maybe half a kilometre, wound its way past a stand of trees, behind which I could just see the top of a house.

When I came around the curve of the trees and into sight of the house, my breath caught. How, in all the years I'd been living on this island, had I never seen this place? It was a dream house, a picture of farmhouse perfection from a half-century ago. I almost expected a woman carrying a tray of lemonade to appear on the porch, and a handful of children to come running around the corner.

Instead, what came around the corner was a tall woman in a gardening apron, her long grey hair pulled back in a ponytail, a stern look on her face, a basket in one hand and garden shears in the other. She was taller than me by several inches, long-limbed in a graceful Katherine Hepburn sort of way. Her face was tanned, feathered with laugh lines around her eyes and at the corners of her mouth. She stood still as could be, waiting.

I cut the engine, the nerves I'd managed to ignore on the drive up here at full force again. I popped my seatbelt, opened the door and stepped out. "Hi there …," I said, realizing with a sudden horror that I had no idea what this woman's name was. David had referred to her only as "my mother." I took a leap, hoping that his last name was also hers, and finished with, "Mrs. March."

She just looked at me, about twenty paces off.

"Your son asked me to come up and meet with you," I said. "So you could interview me?"

Still, silence. I had no idea what to say or do next, so I just stood there, staring back. "Should we—" is all I managed to mumble, and finally she spoke, cutting me off.

"Well, come on, then," she said, and turned to walk back behind the house in the direction she'd just come from. I threw my purse on the seat, locked the car and followed.

Behind the house was a garden that was at least twice as large as Jules's entire apartment, and it was in full harvest-time bloom: green, twisting squash vines; chest-high tomato plants in metal cages; climbing beans on fishnet; tidy rows of carrots, beets and turnips.

"Oh my God," I said. "This is amazing." It came out like a revelatory fact, as though perhaps Mrs. March had never before seen her own garden, and I was filling her in on its magnificence.

She offered me a half smile, handed me a pair of gloves from her garden basket and began to walk up the nearest row. "A garden this big requires a lot of weeding and work," she said, still walking away from me. Without even looking back, she added: "You coming or are you just going to stand there?"

I pulled on the gloves and followed her. At the far end of the row, she kneeled in the dirt, then looked up at me until I did the same. "Start with the obvious weeds between this row and that one," she said. "I need to start pulling carrots and beets."

I started plucking at the bits of green that I guessed were weeds, and watched as she pulled out the vegetables, shaking dirt from them and setting them aside in her basket. "I thought most of these would have been a few weeks back already," I said.

"If you time it right, you can do two harvests. Some things, like the tomatoes, only come through once, but you can get in two rounds of turnips and such."

She said it with her eyes on her work, arms moving without pause.

"Takes a lot of time," she added. "More time than most people have these days. I have the time, so why not?"

I had no idea what to say, so I stayed silent, weeding.

As she moved along the row, I followed, shuffling along on my knees next to her. I thought about asking her some questions, that reverse-interview thing that career experts always say you should do to show you're interested in the job. But every time I looked at her face, she was so focused on the carrots that it seemed a bad idea to interrupt her. So on we went, me finding every wayward weed, her pulling up massive carrots and enormous beets.

Forty-five minutes later, we'd made it to the end of the row, and Mrs. March was standing back up and pulling off her gloves.

"Come on," she said, setting the basket at her feet and striding back around the front of the house.

I did as she said, feeling like a child trailing behind her mother in a grocery store. It was the sort of thing that normally would have irritated me, that I would have complained to Jack over dinner about—someone being rude, the slight of it, the lack of manners—but somehow right then it didn't occur to me to feel that way.

At the front of the house, Mrs. March paused next to my car. "I guess my son has explained everything to you," she said.

I nodded. "Yes, more or less."

"Did he tell you that I don't want to move to Vancouver?" she said.

"No."

"What did he tell you?"

"That my job would be to help you pack up your house," I said, gesturing up at the beautiful home behind her. "And to drive you and your things to BC, to help you with whatever you need along the way, overnight and—"

"Overnight?" She snorted and laughed. "What would you help me with overnight?"

"Sometimes clients need assistance to get out of bed for the bathroom or …."

I let the sentence dangle, my mind a blank. I'd helped clients in the middle of the night do about a million different things, but I'd just watched this woman spend an hour working in her garden—an effort that had left me sweaty, red-faced and breathless, while she seemed as cool and calm as when we'd begun—and it was hard to fathom anything I might do for her that she couldn't do herself. She agreed.

"Well, I assure you, I'm quite capable of taking care of myself *overnight*," she said, emphasizing the word. "David has a very limited vision of what his mother is capable of, apparently."

She stared at me, her lips pressed tight. I wasn't sure what to say, so I just kept quiet. "So why do you want this job?" she asked. "Seems like it'd be a pain-in-the-butt gig."

"I'm between clients," I replied.

She stared at me, expressionless.

"And I have a lot of experience," I added.

She didn't nod or blink or acknowledge my words in any way.

Nervous, I went on with whatever I could think of: "And I've never been past Ontario, so I think it would be nice to see other parts of Canada."

"That's all?" she asked at last.

I opened my mouth and closed it again. Mrs. March stared at me, raised her eyebrows, and waited.

"And … I can't stay here. Because—" I began, and when I looked at her face, there was no judgment, no history, no questions. Suddenly the dam was broken, and it seemed safe to let it all tumble out. "Because I thought I'd be getting married soon, but my ex is with someone else, and I've been living with my best friend, but I can't stay there forever. And … yeah … *that*."

She nodded, then looked past me, her eyes scanning the sky, a calmness on her face, an expression that suggested she was thinking about the pros and cons of a decision. Later, I would realize she was giving me a minute to compose myself, catch my breath and wipe at my eyes.

Finally, she spoke again. "All right. Be back at 8:00 a.m. Bring your things. I'll need you to stay here for the next while before we go—if that's all right with you," she said. "It'll save time on the driving back and forth every day."

"Oh, okay, yes, great," I said. "Anything."

"I don't want to do this," she said, a little more loudly, her eyes pinning mine, like she was fully looking at me for the first time. "Leave, I mean. I don't want to leave my home."

What was there to say to her? I knew how it felt to have to change your life when you don't want to. I didn't really want to leave my "home" either. But here we were, both of us on the verge of doing exactly that. I nodded, silent.

"Okay, then," she said. "I'll see you tomorrow. Ruthie? It's Ruthie, right?"

"Yes, it's Ruthie. Thank you. Thanks, Mrs. March. Thank you."

"Just Kay will do," she said.

"Kay. Thank you."

"Don't thank me yet," she said. "You might want to quit before we get off this island."

I shook my head "no" and smiled.

"We'll see. Tomorrow, 8:00 a.m." She raised her hand, in what could be a wave or a dismissal, and headed back in the direction we'd come from, to her garden.

"Okay! Okay, thanks Kay! See you then! Thank you!"

I was giddy, almost shouting at her as she walked away. I fumbled with my keys, got the door open, plopped down into my seat right on top of my purse, then lifted myself up to pull the purse sideways and onto the passenger seat. My phone inside of it was buzzing, but I ignored it.

I knew the job was mine. Gilbert would give me a great reference, and David had already said it was mine for the taking if I passed muster with his mother. And now, one row of weeding, no questions, one rambling my-life-is-falling-apart confession, and I seemed to have gotten further than all the previous candidates. This was happening. The job I hadn't wanted twenty-four hours ago was mine, and I was ecstatic.

4

Being with Jack had been like being in the centre of the universe. It didn't matter where he was, he always had a good time. He made friends easily, had funny stories to tell and could rally a group of people to enthusiasm over even the dullest of activities. For someone like me, a little shy and introverted, always on the outskirts of the popular crowd in high school, a bit awkward and nerdy, it felt like a kind of magic to be with Jack. All it took was his arm around my shoulder to make me come alive and feel safe enough to tell a joke, to jump into the fun, to suddenly become a louder, more outgoing version of myself.

My parents loved him. After watching me alternate between being single and dating not-quite-right guys, Jack was a dream: stable, normal, fun-loving. Being at family events suddenly felt easier—I was one of the grown-ups, settled, equal to my sister for once.

And I loved saying "we" instead of "me"—if I was invited to something, I could say, "We'll have to look at our calendar," and when people asked what I was doing for the holidays, I'd reply, "We're still thinking about it." My previous boyfriends had always been too flaky, too immature or too disinterested to be the types you made long-term plans with. "We" felt like a badge of maturity and certainty.

And every time something came up, when some compatibility between us was tested or found failing, I shored it up with memories of what it had been like when we first met, the excitement of it all, how that part of us was still there, just maybe a little hidden behind stress about work or bills or life.

It was easy to list all the ways we were well matched: how we wanted the same things, enjoyed the same things and felt the same way about the world, how he made me laugh, how I appreciated his lack of drama, how we never fought.

I loved what I was in his company, but if someone had asked me why I loved him, and how I knew he loved me in return, I'm not sure I'd have had an answer.

✳

I'd taken a slightly circuitous route on my drive home from Kay's, letting my mind wander as I drove, and by the time I'd gotten back to the apartment, there was an email waiting from David:

> Dear Ms. MacInnes,
> I have just spoken with my mother, and she has advised that she considers you a fantastic candidate for the job.

His tone made me chuckle. It was like getting an email from my accountant or lawyer, where the bad news was filtered to sound good. It was much more likely that Kay had said something like "she'll do" or "I guess it's fine" than anything resembling "fantastic candidate." It continued:

> Here are some of my hopes and expectations for the coming weeks:
> 1. All expenses will be covered (food, lodging, gas, incidentals). Obviously, this does not include personal purchases along the way.
> 2. The handover to the new owners of the house is in two weeks. The realtor will deal with this. I will arrange for professional cleaners the day prior to

the hand-off, so please do not worry about deep cleaning beyond the basics. However, all of the household furnishings will need to be dealt with prior to that. All that can come is what fits in the minivan. There is no room here for additional furnishings or large items, so please do not let her ship anything ahead.

3. Once you are on the road heading west, I would like it if you could check in as often as possible by text, phone or Skype, so I am kept up to date on your progress.

4. Ideally, the trip should take no longer than two weeks. The fall weather through the mountain passes between Alberta and BC can turn suddenly, and it would be best to stay ahead of that.

5. Let me know how you would like to do your return travel (air, rail, bus, etc.), and we will make arrangements.

Return travel. I'd forgotten about the coming back part. Of course I wanted to come back; this was my home now. I'd grown up in Quebec, but I'd been here since I'd finished university—which felt, now that I thought about it, like several lifetimes ago. Still, reading the words "return travel" deflated me a little bit. I'd never been past Ontario—never seen the prairies or the Rocky Mountains or the Pacific Ocean. I guess I'd be seeing them just the once and then turning around right away.

6. Please keep in mind that my mother is now seventy-two. She broke her hip and fractured her arm last year. I would prefer that she fly out, but she has insisted on coming by car. Please ensure her safety first and the timeline second. Those are the priorities.

7. All remaining personal expectations—i.e., assistance

with travel, etc.—can be ironed out with my mother as she sees fit, though I may have specific requests along the way.

Ms. MacInnes, as you can probably guess, it's very important to me that my mother arrive here safely. She has been widowed for several years now, and she hasn't yet realized that her isolated living conditions are not the safest environment for her when considering her age. Relocating to my home will be a much safer long-term environment, and I am eager for the trip to be completed, and safely. Please contact me any time with questions, concerns or clarifications.

Yours truly,

David March

Considering how easily Kay had tackled the garden yesterday, not to mention how well she'd dispatched me with a few short words, it didn't seem to me that this was a woman in need of much saving. If anything, she could out-weed—not to mention outrun, out-argue and outwit—me, and I was more than thirty years her junior.

I wanted to say as much to David, if only to put his mind at ease about her "fragile state," but as I closed up my email, I decided it was better not to get involved. They'd obviously sorted this plan out before I came along, and I just needed to do my job: get Kay's house empty in the next two weeks, and then get her and me to the other side of the country before there was snow on the highway.

Simple.

✳

"So, is there a lot still to do at the house?" asked Jules.

I plucked idly at one of the remaining nachos on the plate in front of me. We'd come down to Brewster's—the local pub and hangout—for dinner and a chat before I started packing up my stuff.

"I have no idea. Didn't make it past the driveway and the garden," I replied.

"What if there's a ton of stuff in there? Like, mantelpieces full of knick-knacks and things that her grandkids made that she doesn't want to get rid of?"

Jules and I had spent enough time in clients' homes to know what a lifetime of collecting could look like: very, very crowded. But many older people were forced to downsize from larger homes and reduce their belongings to a fraction just to make it all fit into a small apartment or a basement suite in their adult children's homes. I'd be holding on to my favourite knick-knacks too, I always thought. I'd often taken a few minutes to dust off the tops of figurines, straighten up pictures of grandkids sitting on Santa's knee. For some people, their "stuff" was almost all the company they had in a day, aside from people like me who were hired to come in and do something for them.

"Then I'll tackle that when I get there, I guess," I said. "I don't know; she doesn't strike me as the fussy type, the kind to have a lot of things around. And David is her only son, and I haven't heard any mention of a wife or kids, so not a lot of family."

Now that I thought about it, it was just as likely there *was* a wife and a kid—maybe several kids. We'd only talked about my experience for the job, and the weather; at Kay's I'd been given instructions on how to weed around a row of carrots, and I'd confessed that I had to get away from my crappy ex. There was nothing to indicate that David was flying solo at all. And I'd already scoured the Internet for him: no Facebook profile, no Twitter account, and his company website had no more information about him than I already knew. Just because I hadn't heard about kids didn't mean there weren't any.

"Oh well," said Jules, raising her eyebrows, one corner of her mouth turning up. "That's good news for you, then."

"What?" I asked.

Jules rolled her eyes at me. "You know what."

"What do you mean," I said again, while hunting down the last of the olives on the nacho platter.

"I mean … and you already know this … *Mr. March* is cute. Admit it. And I watched you 'um' and 'oh' and 'hi' your way through that conversation with him, and then giggle—"

"I didn't giggle!"

"And then giggle," she continued, "about the time difference and the weather. I haven't seen you giggle in a *really* long time."

"I didn't giggle," I repeated.

"What's wrong with giggling? Christ, do you have any idea how much time you've spent in your life—and yes, I mean you, we all do it, but you in particular—*not* doing things or doing things based on what you think you're *supposed* to do? Based on what people will think?"

"That's not true."

"It is. It's totally true. Why did you stay with Jack for so long?" she demanded, pointing at me with the tip of one cheese-covered chip.

"Because I loved him." I shrugged.

"Or because he was easy and safe and familiar? Jack was never supposed to be the forever guy."

"Why not?" I said, feeling defensive now. "We loved each other; we worked well together."

"Yep. You did. At one point. You totally did. And then you really probably didn't anymore. How many times have we sat right here, with the same plate of nachos and the same bottles of beer, while you told me about all the ways in which you and Jack were *not* getting along, or that Jack had suggested you take a break from each other, or that it had been three months—*three months*, Ruthie—since you'd had sex with each other. But you stayed and you insisted that he stay too. Because it was simpler than the alternative. Because change terrifies you."

Now I was mad, full-up, straight-out mad. The mention of all the ways my life with Jack hadn't been so great felt like a willful cut in an already open wound.

"Just because some people want to have zero emotional attachments in life and are happy with one unrelated physical connection after another," I began, "doesn't mean we're all happy with that. Some of us want relationships that *mean* something. Relationships we stick with even when they're tough. Some of us don't want to be *just one night* in a long line of fun nights."

Jules stared at me. I was already wishing I could pull the words back in, like a fishing line I'd mis-thrown. For a split second an apology formed on my tongue, but I couldn't speak.

Jules had never had a long-term relationship. Jules had never wanted one, it seemed to me, and she had fun dating casually. I pretended not to get it, watching her go out for a night and return bouncy and cheerful, but deep down it wasn't that I didn't understand—it was that I envied her lack of worry. Jules spent no time wondering if her lack of a "real relationship" was disappointing her family, if the pleasure she took in mutually enjoyable sex with one of her dates was improper or wrong or immoral. She just enjoyed herself. And I resented her for it, on some level.

"Right," said Jules, her face blank now, her smile gone. "Right." She stood up, took a last swig from her bottle of beer and pulled on her jacket. "I've got an early morning. I'm heading back."

She grabbed her purse and walked away, waving to the bartender as she went, and headed straight for the door. Her apartment was only two blocks away. It would take all of five minutes to get home.

Shit. I wanted to feel angry at her, remind myself that she started it. But like the rage I was seeking when I looked at Jack's photos, this anger couldn't be found either. It was just a soft thumping ache, sad and lonely again.

＊

When I got back to the apartment, the door to Jules's bedroom was closed, the soft light of her bedside lamp glowing a semicircle of yellow from under the door. I held my hand up to knock—hesitating, hoping Jules would call my name first—so we could fix it, make it better. The floor creaked under my weight, and a second later the light went out: she'd heard me, knew I was hovering out in the hall, and turned off the light.

I turned back to the living room and saw the two small rolling suitcases I'd purchased on my way home from Kay's. I needed them to pack up my meager belongings. All of my "stuff"—the lamps and the pots and the mugs and such—were still in my old apartment with Jack. The week after I'd found him with Flower Shop Girlfriend, Jules and I had gone back during the day and boxed up all my personal things—framed photos of my family, old files with my university records, financial paperwork—and put them in storage in the basement of Jules's building, locked up with her Christmas decorations and sporting gear. I'd left the household goods; it had been impossible to even consider which items were "mine" after so long together, and all I'd wanted was to finish the task and get out. I'd put my clothes, some jewelry, makeup and small personal items into a garbage bag and left my key on the counter.

Now I needed to pack to leave for Kay's, and it seemed almost as daunting as that day at my old apartment. My things had slowly spread out over Jules's apartment over the last several months, and it took twenty minutes of circling through the kitchen and the living room and the bathroom to round up everything that belonged to me. Half the clothes—all right, fine, *most* of the clothes—needed to be washed. It hadn't seemed such a big deal to re-wear my favourite sweatshirt four days in a row when I wasn't leaving the apartment. Now I wished the smell of spilled wine and sweat was gone, and the wrinkles eased by the heat of the dryer. I'd have to do a few loads at Kay's this week before we started driving.

In the end, I filled one of the suitcases. The second was almost completely empty, except for a pair of sandals and a pair of boots, a hairbrush and a small bag of makeup I had barely touched in months. This was my entire thirty-eight-years-old-and-counting life: not quite two suitcases of stuff, and a few boxes tucked away in a basement.

At least it was easy to pack, I told myself as I lay down on the couch and pulled the blankets up. If nothing else, I had accomplished this much: a very transportable life.

5

WHEN I WOKE in the morning, Jules was already gone. I was relieved in a way: if I'd had to look her in the face right now, I'd have been doubly ashamed. And if she pretended it hadn't happened, I'd get sappy and emotional trying to say goodbye. I showered, dressed in a pair of leggings and a sweatshirt, laced up my sneakers and pulled my bags to the door.

I walked back to the kitchen and found a pen and pad of paper. I stared at it for a full two minutes, trying to come up with something good to say. In the end, I wrote: *I love you. Thank you for the couch. And everything else. I'm sorry I'm a bitch sometimes when I'm scared.*

It sounded good as I wrote it, but when I scanned it after I wrote it, I saw exactly what she would. A vague apology that was trying to divert fault: *It's not me; it's just my fear. I'm not an asshole; I'm just worried. You can't hold it against me personally; it's just that bad things have happened to me.* It was lame. But I was out of time to rewrite, and I didn't have the energy to think about it anyway.

I pulled my suitcases out into the hallway, locked the door and then slipped my spare key back underneath, hard enough that it would be sitting a good two or three feet in front of the door when Jules arrived home from work later. I took a deep breath and headed to the stairs.

✳

"Well, I suppose all of this will need to be boxed up and given away," Kay said, pointing at the upper shelves in the kitchen. Plates, mixing bowls, a sea of mismatched mugs.

"You could try to sell it? Put something up on Craigslist?"

"No, I don't want to bother. I don't need the money anyway, and we're out of time."

"We could bring it to the women's shelter in town. I saw something on the news about them; they help women from abusive relationships get back on their own feet. They probably could use household stuff for some of the families?"

"Perfect. Do that, please. Use the van, though—it'd take a hundred trips in your little thing."

I started to pull the plates down onto the counter, thinking of how many trips it might still take, even in the van. There was a lot here, a lifetime of things that had been used for dinners and parties and tea in the afternoon. Kay emptied a cutlery drawer, wrapping things up in sheets of newspaper as she went.

When I'd cleared all the shelves in the cupboard, I realized there were a few larger items sitting above the cupboard, too far out of reach to get to easily. I dragged a chair over, climbed up onto it and reached up, feeling around blindly.

"It'll be easier if you get right up on the counter," said Kay, pointing up. "I don't think there's much up there but dust bunnies, but it's worth the check, I suppose."

I grabbed the edge of the cupboard and stepped up from the chair to the counter, coming eye level to the upper edge, then peered around once I felt steady.

"Oh, there are a few things up here, actually," I said.

Kay came over, and I handed the items down to her one at a time. A casserole dish with the familiar CorningWare blue flowers on its side, a round cookie tin edged with rust, a darkened baking sheet. Kay added each of them to the box for donations.

"Here, one more thing," I said, reaching as far to the right as

I could to grab the nearest edge of a thin wooden box. I pulled it toward me, then handed it down to Kay. "Not sure what this is."

Kay took it in both hands and lowered it slowly to the counter. "It's a cribbage board."

She reached into the sink for a damp cloth and wiped the layer of dust off the board while I hopped back down to the chair, then to the floor.

"Here, I'll add it to one of the donation boxes," I said, extending a hand to take it back from her.

"No." She turned the board over, wiping down the back of it. In the bottom right corner, there was lettering—I couldn't tell if it was done with paint or carved into the wood, but I could make out what was there: BWK 1968.

"BWK?" I asked, trying to get a better look.

"A friend," she answered, still wiping at the grime. "A friend made this for me."

"Oh."

"This is coming with us," she said.

"Okay."

"I'm not getting rid of it." She held it close, still wiping at its surface with the cloth, her head down, focused intently on the task.

"Sure. Of course. It's up to you."

Kay hadn't looked at me once as she spoke, but she held the board in her hands now, and I could see that the polished wood shone. Three tracks of holes ran in parallel around the centre of the board. I knew enough about cribbage to know that this was where the pegs went, keeping score as you played and earned points. Beyond that, I couldn't remember much about how the game was played.

Around the outside edges, carved evergreens stood out in relief, the small slashes that must have been made with a knife marking out the branches and trunk. At the corners, small pine cones were etched into the wood. At one end, a sun was rising over the mountains, and at the other end, the wood had been carved into a crescent moon and stars.

Kay ran her fingers across the top of the board, feeling the edges of the mountain, the points on the stars.

"It's really beautiful," I said. "Do you want me to bring it to the 'keep' pile?"

"No, I'll pack it," Kay answered. "Just keep on in here, okay?" She waved her hand around in the general direction of the sink and cupboards, still not looking at me.

"Okay," I said.

She left the kitchen, her footfalls echoing up the hallway to the front room, then beyond to her bedroom. After a few minutes, the front screen door creaked open and slammed closed. A moment later, I saw her through the kitchen window as she came around the side of the house. She wandered over to the garden, walked down the row of tomatoes, pausing here and there to check the fruit on the vine, then continued on past the garden toward a stand of trees another hundred metres beyond. I hadn't been back there, but Kay had mentioned a creek that went through, and it looked from here to be a pretty little spot to go for a bit of shade on a warm afternoon. Kay followed the path into the trees and, in a few seconds, disappeared from sight.

I started for the washroom down the hall to wash up. As I passed Kay's bedroom, I saw the crib board sitting on the foot of her bed, next to her open suitcase. I wanted to sneak in and look at it again, examine the detail on the pine cones and the trees, turn it over and run my fingers over the initials etched in the back. It felt like an invasion to do so, like looking at someone's photo album without their permission, so I carried on to the washroom. There was still lots of work to do, and time was running out to get it all done.

*

I woke up in darkness as solid as tar. I was used to the streetlights in town, the light sneaking in around curtains and blinds. But out here at Kay's, night was a deep darkness, and silent except for the random owl during the night and the birds at dawn.

But as I came up out of sleep, I heard something new: a faint snuffling noise, like a small child catching her breath after a fall from a tree. I sat up and followed the noise into the kitchen; the back door was open a few inches, and the noise was coming from outside on the step.

I hesitated for a second—town brain wondered if we'd been broken into, but country brain reminded me that we were miles from anyone, and Kay rarely locked the doors to begin with. I put my hand to the door and opened it a crack more.

Kay was sitting on the back step, facing out toward the garden and the woods beyond. A sliver of a crescent moon provided just enough light to see the outline of her head and shoulders, picking up the silvery strands in her hair. She sniffed, twice, and ran her hand over her face to wipe at tears.

"Are you going to stand there looking at me, or are you going to come out and look at the stars?" she asked, her voice soft and gentle in a way it never was during the day as she orchestrated the packing and preparing.

I pushed the door open enough to step out; the back porch was cool on my feet as I crossed to sit down on the step next to her. She didn't move at all, not a nod or a word in my direction. It felt like an interruption of whatever she was doing to even sit here, let alone ask any questions in the dark quiet, so I just kept silent.

She pointed up at the sky. The stars were, indeed, stunning. I'd seen them like this as a little girl, but it had been decades since I'd managed to get a glimpse like this: the full spray of stars splashed out across the sky, a thousand, million, billion pinpricks of light. It made me feel small, but in a good way. In the grand expanse of the universe, of all the things that could happen to a person, how bad was what had happened to me? I was alive. What else could one ask for, considering the chances of even that having occurred in the first place?

Kay's breath hitched, and I looked at her out of the corner of my eye. There was just enough light to see that she'd begun to cry again. I pretended not to notice and sat as still as I could. In a moment, the hitch had turned to quiet sobs, and after a moment—as though she'd just decided it wasn't worth the effort necessary to keep it in—the sobs grew louder and longer, so she had to take huge gulps of air to keep up to the uncontrollable outburst. It was so unlike anything I'd seen in the few days I'd known Kay that I was frozen, uncertain what to do.

Jules had sat next to me just a few nights before, when I'd given in to the same need. It had helped to have a witness, somehow, even though it felt shameful too. It made it real to know that my pain was seen. And when Jules reached out to comfort me like a mother might, it had touched some deep wounded part of me. She couldn't fix that part; only I could, by letting it scar over. But she had eased my hurt, in the moment.

As Kay's shoulders shook, with her face in her hands almost resting on her knees, I reached out my hand to her back, as Jules had done for me. "Shh, it's okay, it'll be okay," I whispered, repeating the words again and again, a dozen times over.

I couldn't tell if she'd even heard me. She continued, unabated, for several more minutes until suddenly, she stopped. After another minute, she raised her head from her hands and used the collar of her nightshirt to wipe her face.

"Getting old is shit, you know," she said at last.

I had no idea what the right answer was, so I didn't say anything at all.

"Half of my friends are already dead. Some that are still alive are in homes, with dementia and worse. The rest are like me:

widowed or soon to be and suddenly a burden on our kids, whether we want to be or not."

She was silent a moment and shook her head side to side.

"David's not wrong. It's not safe for me here anymore," she looked at me then. "Do you know how that feels? To admit that your own body might not safely take you in and out of the bath? That you could hurt yourself and there's no one nearby to help? That you can't keep up with the little repairs and the work and the garden and all of the other things that five or ten years ago you did without batting an eye?" She paused, sighed. "I'm so tired, Ruthie."

I frowned. Of all the words I might have used to describe this woman, "tired" was absolutely not one of them. She looked out at the garden and half smiled.

"I loved this place. I still love it. But even here wasn't really home. Not truly. I think I only ever felt like I was home in one place in my entire life ...," she trailed off.

I wanted to know more, but I didn't dare ask what she meant.

"Every single huge change in my life was out of my control. Every single one. Including this. And what's the point in fighting it—what's the point in being sad, even?" She shrugged her shoulders. "Almost all of my choices haven't really been my choice. What's one more?"

She stood up, brushed off her rear end and turned back to the door. "We'd better get to bed, Ruthie. We have a lot of work this week."

The door creaked open and closed, and she disappeared inside the house. I sat a moment longer, looking at the milky wash of stars over the black of the sky, the inky outline of treetops in the distance, the glint of moonlight off a window on a barn beyond that. Eventually I pulled myself up and followed Kay inside.

✳

Five days later, the work was done. We'd used a dozen rolls of packing tape and an endless pile of newspapers, and we'd both broken more than one fingernail along the way, but we'd managed to finish it. A stack of boxes waited in the front landing, with a second pile of luggage and personal items next to it. A rain jacket was tucked through the handle of the suitcase, with odds and ends balanced here and there, all ready to load into the minivan.

The rest of the house was empty, every room bare, every shelf clear. Kay and I had slept that last night on the living room floor on a pair of twin mattresses that had been in one of the spare rooms. When we woke, we stripped the bedding and waited for the family up the road to come and pick them up—their toddler twins were almost old enough to move into "big boy" beds, and Kay had offered them to grateful acceptance.

I'd driven my car back into town two nights earlier and parked it outside the Just Like Family office, with Gilbert's approval that I could leave it there for a few weeks. Kay had followed me in the van, and we'd returned in silence, watching the familiar landscape roll by.

After the beds were gone, Kay grabbed the Coleman cooler and announced that she was going to pack up the last of the items in the fridge; she suggested I could start loading the van.

"Let's just get it done and get on the road," Kay said.

I could tell she was in no mood for chit-chat, so I got to work, pulling the van around and backing it in as close to the door as possible. I stacked boxes in the back, then on the rear seats, then filled in the empty spots with random items, a jigsaw puzzle of odds and ends, trying to get everything in. Our own personal bags were kept close to the sliding side door so that they'd be easy to unload into the hotel at the end of each day.

At last it was done, and I wandered back inside.

"Here, this is ready," Kay said, pointing at the cooler. I grabbed it and lugged it out to the van, depositing it just inside the sliding door so we could get to it easily at pit stops. When Kay didn't follow me out, I went back in to see what was holding her up.

She was still standing in front of the fridge, the door wide open, the light on inside.

"Kay?"

"Hmm? Yes, I know. I'm coming. I'm being sentimental and silly is all. Just give me a sec."

She stood still a moment longer, then closed the door.

"Oh, we forgot one," I said, pointing to the front of the fridge door, a lone magnet still on it.

"That's fitting," Kay said, plucking it off the fridge and holding it up. "Vancouver."

It was a small photo of the city lit up at night, the Lions Gate Bridge strung with lights.

"Beautiful," I said.

"It is, yes. David sent me this when he moved there, years ago."

I tried to picture David in Vancouver. I'd spoken to him the night before for a few minutes after he'd finished talking with his mother. We'd gone over the last of the arrangements: the cleaners, the house sale. His voice had been tight and tired, no hint of the humour that I'd seen in our interview. He had reviewed the travel plans several times, the details highlighted over and over again with the word "safe"—which route was safe, which hotels were safe, his concern about how safe the old van might or might not be.

I answered at the appropriate times—"got it, absolutely, will do, I totally understand"—though I didn't think he was really listening to me by then, and just before we hung up, he sighed. "I wish she'd just fly, for God's sake. I don't know why I agreed to this."

I'd looked over at Kay just then and could tell by the way she held herself that she could hear most, if not all, of the conversation through the phone.

"You don't know why *you* agreed to this?" she whispered under her breath and shook her head.

"David," I said, my voice louder than necessary, "I think I've got everything. We've got it covered. It's good. Okay? We'll be in touch when we're settled the first night."

He'd given three or four more instructions while I bit my tongue, wanting to defend Kay; when he hung up, Kay scoffed, and then I felt an equal urge to defend David. She *is* capable, I wanted to tell him. He just *worries,* I wanted to say to her. But she left the room before I could offer an opinion that wasn't mine to give.

✳

I took one last look at the magnet, then turned and left the kitchen, heading for the door. Behind me, Kay jangled her keys, pulling off the ones for the house, which we'd been instructed to leave in a special lockbox provided by the realtor.

We stood on the doorstep as she locked up, and I waited for Kay to say something or get choked up, but when the keys were secured, she simply turned her back to the house and strode to the van. I raced to catch up.

"Vancouver-bound, then," she said, and smiled at me. She put the magnet on the hood of the van, smack dab in the middle.

"It'll fall off," I said.

"I bet it won't," she replied.

I disagreed but shrugged. Her van, her magnet, her loss. I closed the rear door, slammed the sliding door shut and hopped in the front seat. Suddenly, the notion of being away from here—from my ex, from the drinking, even from Jules, oddly—was thrilling in a way I had not expected. I was ready to go. More than ready to go, it seemed. I turned the key in the ignition, and as I felt the rumble of the old van shake up my arms through the steering wheel, I felt like I might burst. I'd be off this island by noon, with an entire country ahead of me.

I peeked over at Kay. She did not look as enthusiastic as I felt. What I wanted to say was: Look, there's no such thing as ready when it comes to someone else deciding you ought to change your entire life. Ready was for people who had set out on a path, who had pointed and said, 'There, that thing, let's do that.' But let's just pretend and get going. Instead, I sniffed and asked: "Ready?"

She put her shoulders back and nodded. "Ready as I'll ever be, I suppose. Let's go."

I tried not to watch her, but I couldn't help it, keeping her in my peripheral vision all the way up the long driveway to the road. She didn't look back, or cry, or even furrow her brow. She stared straight ahead. I wanted to touch her shoulder as I had that night on the porch, say something kind, at least acknowledge that I understood this was hard—and that "hard" was a poor word to even begin to sum it all up—but I knew she'd scoff and shake it off.

As we turned onto the paved road that would take us up to Highway 1, the rigid line of Kay's shoulders eased, and she sat back in her seat, head turned to the window. "So I have some … ideas. About the trip. Just a few changes to the plan. Nothing major."

"Sure," I replied, distracted by the weaving traffic ahead of me. "What kind of changes?"

"I'll tell you over breakfast." Her body was still turned toward the window, her head angled away from me, but even so I was sure I caught—in the very edge of my vision—the corner of her mouth turning up in a grin. "Don't worry. It'll be fun."

6

I LOOKED AT the menu as though it might contain the secret to
life, but I didn't really want anything on offer. I was starving,
sure, but in the back of my mind, I was wondering if it was too
early for a glass of wine. I hadn't had a drink since I'd been at
Kay's. I'd been so busy with packing and cleaning that I hadn't
had time to think about Jack or Jules or anything else, and by bedtime I'd been so exhausted that I was dead to the world in minutes
despite being sober. It had been the first time in months that I'd
slept so easily. But a single morning of driving—with nothing to
distract me from old memories—had swallowed up the excitement I'd felt pulling out of Kay's driveway and replaced it with a
sense of familiar dread and sadness.

"Right," I said, slapping the menu shut. "Omelette it is. And a
coffee. Or like, six coffees, maybe."

Kay was staring at me, hands resting on the tabletop, menu
aside. I stared back. She cocked her head. Was I supposed to say
something? Ask a question? She raised her eyebrow, like she was
waiting on me, and I opened my mouth once but then closed it
again. If I'd learned anything at all in the last weeks with Kay, it
was that she'd talk when she wanted to, and not before.

"So," she said.

I looked sideways, praying that the waitress would come and
intervene—plus, I really needed that coffee, even more than I needed
the wine, which on the balance seemed positive.

But the waitress was on the far side of the diner, chatting to a pair of guys who were likely taking a break from their long-haul routes. The parking lot was full of huge semi-trailers, our mini-van like a cute little baby elephant tucked in amongst the giants.

"So," Kay said again. "Here's the plan."

She pushed a slip of paper across the table toward me.

The plan? We already had a plan. David had sent the itinerary to me by email several days ago. It was beautiful and excruciating in its detail. How many miles to cover each day, what hotel to stop at each night, with a list of the amenities and nearby restaurants for meals. He had helpfully included a handful of sightseeing pit stops along the way that he felt might interest his mother, since she *insisted on driving for the sightseeing*, he'd written—though to be honest, I wasn't sure there was time for any of them to fit into his precision schedule.

"But—" I started.

"Yes, I know. David's 'Very Important Itinerary,'" she said, her fingers waggling air quotes while she rolled her eyes. "There are some things I'd like to do. Things that aren't on my son's list."

"But—"

"Yes, I know. You feel like David is your boss, and he's told you what to do and you ought to do it. But I'm your boss, actually."

"But—" I stammered a third time, beginning to feel like an idiot.

"Your boss. And ... your friend," she said, her defiant stare flickering then, a hesitation creeping into her eyes. "And this is important to me."

She looked down at her hands. Her fingers were interlaced, and I could see she was gripping them tightly, worrying. "Just ... read it, please."

I set the menu aside and picked up the paper. Foolscap—old-school yellow, lined paper. At the top, in pencil: Road Trip Checklist. That was underlined, twice, then below it, a numbered list:

1. Show Ruthie the list (*argue?)
2. Don't cry when crossing Confederation Bridge
3. Read (or reread) three Canadian writers
4. Write a poem
5. Stand in the Pacific Ocean
6. Get drunk (shots?)
7. Take a photo at every provincial border
8. Steal something
9. Stop at the Continental Divide (can we? where is it?)
10. Visit the cottage at Sand Bay again
11. Visit Drumheller
12. Swim as often as possible
13. Go dancing
14. Buy a piece of local art along the way
15. Meet new people
16. See the highest tide (*penis rock)
17. Watch the sun set or rise on a mountaintop in BC
18. Visit a big XXX store and buy something fun
19. New hairdo
20. Have great sex at least once
21. _____

Number 2 was already crossed off, a single line through it. The last one was empty, as though leaving room to add new ideas. Some items were so small and minor that it seemed silly to list them at all; others were … well, others were going to be a little more challenging, if not impossible.

And it would take a heck of a lot longer than David's "Very Important Itinerary" would allow.

"Kay," I started, but then stopped, looking at the list again.

"Look, I want to tell you it's not up to you, that I'm the boss and here's how it's going to be. But we have to be partners in this, and I know that David wants you to get me there in exactly

8.75 days or whatever it is he's determined it should take. But I've agreed to go, and I think I get some say in how."

She took a deep breath and squared her shoulders.

"Why—" I started, not sure if I wanted to ask why she was going in the first place or why she wanted to do the things on the list or why she wasn't good at insisting or some other why altogether. She shook her head and held up her hand.

"Let's just … drive. And see how *it* goes," she said, motioning to the list. "We can get as many as possible; we'll fit them in. We'll tell David I get tired easily from the driving, that it's taking longer than you thought. Lord knows he'll believe it; he thinks I'm on death's doorstep as it is."

I frowned.

"Is there something you need to get back sooner for?" Her face was the picture of innocence.

"No, but—" my eyes darted back to the list. Get drunk. Have sex. Visit the cottage. What cottage? And steal something? It was equal parts sightseeing tour and sin-seeking, with a dash down memory lane.

She took the list back from me, laid it flat on the table and smoothed her hand across it, fingers trailing over the wrinkled paper. "Please, Ruthie."

I took a deep breath. She didn't want to be doing this any more than I did. But here we were, two boats bobbing together on a big empty ocean, pushed together by currents we couldn't control. Would we let the tide take us where it would? Or should we put up the sail and decide where we were heading ourselves? I held my hands out for the paper, and she handed it back. I looked over it one more time. Nodded. "Okay. We're doing it."

Kay beamed, and I swear she bounced and wiggled in her seat. I'd just figure out how to tell David later. Much, much later.

✳

I got as far as the parking lot before David called.

"Hello?"

"Hi! Ruth? It's David. I just wanted to check in. See how things are going. Everything okay so far? How's the driving? Mom doing okay?" He barely took a breath between one question and the next.

"Yes, it's all good, everything is great, fine. Of course. Yes."

Did I sound jumpy? I did. I definitely sounded sketchy. And guilty. I hadn't even done anything yet.

"So you will be in Fredericton by tonight, yes? You can just send me a text when you get there, maybe, and let me know."

"Yeah, that's the plan but ... well, your mom wanted to stop at Hopewell Rocks, so I think we might do that."

Okay, this seemed safe. A diversion, yes, but a David-approved one.

He was silent for a moment. "Oh yeah. Okay, well, sure, I guess that's good. Haven't been there in a long time, but it is beautiful. And it's not far off your route. Mom will like it. But you'll check in, yes?"

"Yep. Totally. I will check in."

"Okay. Good."

There was silence over the line, and I heard a *bing* in the background, like maybe he'd just received an email on his computer. I imagined he was sitting at his desk, and I remembered how he'd looked sitting in his office while he'd interviewed me. Jules had called him cute, but he wasn't really, not in the way that might draw someone's attention in a crowd. Not in a flirty, handsome way.

The only word that came to mind was compelling. He was compelling, to me. He had beautiful eyes, certainly. I'd noticed a small scar on his jawline, and his nose was slightly bent—broken once upon a time, maybe. I wanted to look at him again, carefully, like a scientist.

"Ruth, I just want to say ... it's great ... well, I'm really glad this all came together."

"Me too. I like your mother's company; she's fun."

"Yeah, she's more fun than me, probably," he said, a small laugh evident in his tone. He was much more relaxed than the night before, when he'd rattled off instructions about safety. "She can be pretty stubborn though."

"Sometimes," I said, noncommittal. It seemed disloyal to Kay, after our conversation over breakfast, to say more than that.

I looked over at Kay. She was leaning over the hood of the minivan, map laid out. She must have picked it up in the gas station attached to the diner when she'd gone over for gum. I couldn't remember the last time I'd seen an actual honest-to-goodness paper map. I used my phone for things like that. She pulled the yellow paper out of her pocket and unfolded it on top of the map, like she was orienting herself to line both of them up. A treasure map and the list of treasures. She looked up at me and smiled, a huge grin, and her eyebrows went up and down like she was a comedian telling the punchline of a joke.

It was the first real smile I'd seen her give. The others before now were perfunctory, polite, necessary. But this smile—this huge, thrilling smile—was real. She was excited. I grinned back, a burst of energy shooting through me, a glow of warmth.

"Ruth, thank you. It's really great to have someone I trust doing this. I know I don't know you very well, but … I trust you," David said through the phone.

My stomach did a loop-de-loop. Shit. He wasn't just saying it; he really did trust me. And I had just promised his mother that his well-planned itinerary was out the window in favour of her crazy last-chance road trip checklist. Shit. Shit. Shit.

I cleared my throat, looked away from Kay, and made my voice sound as confident as possible.

"Thank you. You don't need to worry about us; we'll get there safe and sound. I promise."

"Have a good drive today, Ruth. Give my mom a hug for me.

If she'll let you," he said, chuckling.

"Will do. Ciao."

I hung up quickly before he could say anything else.

"All right," I said, heading toward Kay. "Let's do this. Bay of Fundy, Hopewell Rocks, right?"

Kay nodded.

"Awesome," I said, nodding back like we'd just made a deal. "It's supposed to be beautiful there."

"It is. But even better, there's a rock there that looks like a huge penis. I want a picture of us standing next to it."

"A penis rock."

"Yep."

I took a deep breath. "Just what I was hoping for today," I sighed. "A huge penis. Made out of rock. Fantastic."

Kay laughed and went around to the passenger side of the car. "Here we go," she said.

"Here we go," I echoed, under my breath.

7

THE THING ABOUT Jack was that he had fit the bill *well enough*. He was smart enough and reliable enough and handsome enough. But at first, he was more than just "enough"—to me, he was movie-star handsome, funny and brilliant, and being with him made me part of an inner circle I hadn't even realized I wanted to be part of. I belonged, suddenly, and it was intoxicating. And if, over the years, my assessment of him had shifted, if the veneer was tarnished, I was able to ignore it in exchange for the familiarity and safety he provided. Like Jack himself, our relationship was good enough too.

Until it wasn't. Until I was standing naked in the middle of my apartment, looking down at Jack and Flower Shop Girl. Until I'd thrown my clothes on, stormed out of the apartment and waited for him to chase after me, and he hadn't. Until I had to tell my parents that there would be no wedding, no house and garden, no children. It wasn't until much later that it occurred to me they'd long since realized that the wedding-house-children trifecta wasn't in the works. Jack cheating on me was just the nail in the lid of a coffin we'd already been lying in for ages. Sometimes I wasn't sure what was worse: being betrayed by Jack or the fact that no one was surprised when it happened, and not because he was a bad guy, but just because any fire we'd had was long since gone—and everyone else saw it but me.

"Asshole," I muttered.

"What's that?" Kay asked from the seat next to me.

"Oh, sorry … I was just letting my mind wander."

"To assholes?"

"Yep." I nodded firmly.

"One in particular, or assholes in general?"

"Mostly one in particular." I looked out the window, hoping she'd leave it alone. She didn't.

"Want to talk about it?"

"Not really."

"Okay."

I was silent for a full minute, then blurted: "He cheated on me."

"You said that the day we met, yes."

"Which is pretty much the biggest relationship-asshole move there is, right?"

"Yes. I guess so."

I looked over at her, narrowed my eyes, shook my head. "No. It is. Not maybe. It is."

"Things are rarely black and white."

"Some things are. Rolling around nude with someone is pretty black and white. Cheating on your partner is pretty black and white. Being an asshole is pretty black and white."

Kay didn't answer.

I looked over at her again. "This is the part where you're supposed to agree with me. He's an asshole."

Kay pointed at a sign ahead of us.

"Next exit. Hopewell Rocks," she said.

Fine, I thought. Don't agree with me. But he is an asshole.

I put my clicker on and turned off the highway. It really was beautiful country, though it had been years since I'd taken much more than a five-minute pit stop when travelling through this region. "I've never been to Hopewell Rocks. I've driven through Moncton, like, a million times to go home to see my family, but I've never taken the time to go see the rocks."

"Where's your family?"

"In Quebec. Shawville. It's a small town; you probably don't know it."

"I know it. I lived in Ottawa for a time, before we came to PEI. Before David was born. A friend of mine had a cottage near there, in Sand Bay."

"Really? In Sand Bay? Jeez, small world."

"Didn't you notice Sand Bay on my list?"

"No," I said, shaking my head. "Oh, the cottage thing? I guess I did see it, but I didn't make the connection."

I'd skimmed the list for highlights but hadn't absorbed the details. Sand Bay was where most of the kids I grew up with went in the summertime, to cottages dotting along small lakes and the Ottawa River. I'd spent plenty of time there myself, joining my cousins at their place when school was out.

Kay pulled out her list and unfolded it. "Number 10: Visit the cottage in Sand Bay again."

"Oh, well, it's sort of along the way, I guess."

"If your parents are in Shawville, we sure as heck aren't leaving Quebec without going to say hi—and then we'll check off #10 at the same time."

I didn't really want to see my parents, but that was an argument that could wait till later. "What do we need to do there—will it take a lot of time? Are you visiting someone you know in Sand Bay?"

"No. It won't take any time at all. I just want to see it again, that's all."

I wanted to ask why, but the way she turned her head to look out the window made it clear she was already done talking about it.

❋

We hiked down the path to the beach at Hopewell Rocks. School was back in, so the masses of summer tourists who'd no doubt been here just a few weeks back were thinned out to a quiet crowd.

It was warm and sunny, the air salty. It felt like home—but just different enough to remind me that I was no longer home now.

"This is the highest tide in the world?" I asked Kay as we paused at an informational sign. "Huh. Who knew?"

"I did."

I rolled my eyes at her. "All right then. What else am I ignorant about?"

"Where should I start? You're a babe in the woods, my dear. You don't even know how much you don't know yet."

I barked out a laugh. "I'm thirty-eight. That's basically middle age. I'm not exactly a teenybopper."

"Yeah. Well, come back and talk to me after menopause, and we'll see how you feel then."

Menopause. I blinked. Yes, I guess it wasn't so far away, really. And here I was, the childless spinster extraordinaire. I sighed.

Kay chuckled at the sound of it and paused to look back at me. "Oh, for heaven's sake, Ruthie. Are you going to feel sorry for yourself this entire trip?"

She turned and kept walking down the path. I watched her go for a minute, then hurried to catch up.

"I don't feel sorry for myself," I said.

"Yes, you do."

"How do you know? I haven't even told you anything about—"

"You don't need to. I can see it in your face. In the way you walk. The way you listen. Like you're waiting for more bad things. If you're always watching for the next bad thing, you'll miss the good things in between."

"Thanks for the clichés, but I'm good. Really."

"All right then. If you say so." Kay shrugged and picked up her pace again. As we finally reached the beach, she turned back at me and grinned. "See?" she asked, pointing across the clearing of wet sand. "Penis rock."

I followed the line of her finger, then started to laugh. "Oh my

God. It actually is. That's hilarious."

A phallic column of rough rock protruded up from the ground, as though a stone giant had been buried under the sand and all that remained showing was his enormous erection and testicles as he lay on his back. I couldn't stop laughing, giggling like a kid who'd just seen something naughty. Kay beamed at me, like she was pleased that she'd shown me something that made me smile, at last.

"All right," I said. "Go stand next to it so I can take a picture. We have to get back on the road. David wants us to make it to Fredericton tonight. We've got a drive ahead of us yet."

Kay marched over to the rock and flung her arms around it.

"You're a pervert!" I called.

She laughed. "Yes, I am. Or I was. Once upon a time."

"Oh, that sounds like a story I need to hear."

She just shrugged again. "My secrets are all very boring," she said.

I suspected that the opposite was true; in fact, it seemed to me that there was more to know about Kay than I might learn in six trips across the country, let alone just one. I took a few photos of her on my phone, and then she made me switch places with her. I stood awkwardly next to it.

"Come on, Ruthie. Hug the penis. Embrace the penis. Love the penis." Each time she said the word "penis," she said it louder than the time before, until she was yelling PENIS at me. A small group of retirees looked over, and I motioned with my hand for Kay to shush.

"Aren't you glad we came?" she shouted at me. "When was the last time you had such a huge, literally rock-hard cock in arm's reach?"

My mouth fell open. Did she just yell "cock" in front of a bunch of senior citizens? All right, so *she* was a senior citizen herself, technically. But still. "Kay!"

She laughed and handed me back the phone as I approached.

"Okay, let's go," I said, trying to hustle her away before anyone got grumpy.

We hoofed back up the hill and toward the small tourist building.

"I want to take a look at the gift shop," she said, pointing through the door. "Why don't you go ahead to the car, and I'll be there in a minute."

I shrugged. "Sure, okay."

I walked through the shop and out into the parking lot, following a few feet behind a young couple who were walking with their clasped hands swinging between them.

Newlyweds, I bet, I thought to myself, rolling my eyes at their cheeriness. *Ugh.* He probably leaves his underpants on the floor every single morning, I imagined. And she probably insists on watching *The Bachelor,* even when an important hockey game is on. Good luck with your happy marriage.

I unlocked the car, slid into the driver's seat and scrolled through the photos we'd just taken, my hand swiping harder than necessary. It felt good to have a small bit of anger in me, just then, and I held on to it as I scanned the pictures.

The ones of Kay were great. A huge grin, enthusiasm. Then mine: Kay had taken about two dozen photos in quick succession, so that scrolling through them felt like watching an old stop-motion movie. Me, walking to the penis rock. Me, awkwardly standing next to the penis rock. Me, exclaiming with mouth wide open over Kay's use of the word "cock." I looked unhappy. And old. When did I get so old?

"Fantastic," I said to myself under my breath, just as the passenger side door flew open and Kay—breathless and frantic—jumped in the car.

"Go! Go, go, go. Drive, let's go. Let's go, Ruthie! Now!"

I turned the key, started the engine and put it into drive.

"Faster, Ruthie! Come on!"

I put my foot on the gas pedal and circled out of the parking lot. "Kay, what the fuck, what did you do?"

She was leaning back in the seat now, catching her breath, smiling.

She reached down into the pocket of her long flannel shirt. "I got us a souvenir," she said with a smile. She opened her hand to show me two Hopewell Rocks magnets. "For the car. We'll add them to the other one," she pointed out the window at the magnet she'd stuck to the hood as we left the house. "See, it's still there."

"Kay, did you pay for those?"

"Well—"

"No, not 'well' … did you pay for them or not?"

"Ruthie—"

"Did you *pay* for them, Kay? Yes or no."

"No."

My hands gripped the steering wheel. "Are you kidding? Are you fourteen years old? What are you thinking?"

"The list, Ruthie. An opportunity presented itself, and I had to be bold," she said. "Number 8. Steal something. Check!"

I glared at her. She looked relaxed and pleased with herself. Then the *chirp-chirp* of a police siren blared out behind us. I looked in the rear-view mirror: we were being pulled over.

✳

"Do you know how fast you were going?"

I looked up at the police officer and squinted, the sun behind him blinding me. "No, I don't know. I was, well, I guess I was just … I'm not sure," I mumbled. "Was it quite fast?"

"Yes, it was quite fast. But that's not why I pulled you over."

I looked at Kay and pressed my lips together. This was her fault. She'd stolen the magnets, and someone had obviously seen her and called the police. We were going to be arrested and probably end up in jail. I was going to have to call David. How was I going to explain this?

"Okay, look, so—" I started.

"Your rear brake light isn't working, driver's side," he said. "You need to get it fixed."

"Oh," I said.

I looked at Kay. Maybe he didn't know about the thievery.

"How far are you driving, ladies?"

Kay leaned over me and said: "To Vancouver."

"That's a long trip. You should get this sorted out right away," he said, motioning toward the rear of the car.

"Yes, we will. We'll get it done first thing tonight or tomorrow morning. I promise," I said.

"Good," he said, and smiled.

Oh, thank goodness, I thought. No arrest.

He leaned over to smile into the car at Kay, and that's when his eyes flickered down to the cup holders between the front seats. His eyes narrowed, and his smile disappeared.

"Ladies, can you please exit the vehicle."

What the hell? I scanned my eyes down in the direction he had looked. A glass pot pipe was nestled in the cup holder. How had I possibly not seen that? I glared at Kay and mouthed, "What the fuck?" She shrugged, but to her credit did not laugh. Her face was ashen, and her smile was gone.

"Ladies, now. I do not want to ask again."

We opened the doors and climbed out of the car.

"Please wait at the side of the road," he said, motioning us away from traffic.

My phone buzzed in my hand. A text. From David. "Jesus Christ," I whispered. I shoved the phone in my pocket and crossed my arms.

✳

It took seven hours and forty-five minutes—give or take—to have the car towed to the police station for a full search, carry out a second sobriety test, get a stern talking-to by the police officer about travelling with a controlled substance in the car and driving under the influence, and then be released again. My rear end hurt from sitting on the bench in the police station all night.

"Sorry," Kay said, for about the tenth time.

"It's fine."

"I really am sorry. I didn't even think of it! It's just pot, and it's not illegal, and I hardly ever even smoke it. It was just ... there."

Aside from the pipe in the cup holder, there was a small Ziploc baggie of pot in the glovebox, along with a few packs of Zig-Zag rolling papers and several lighters. The police hadn't even confiscated any of it—but they had needed to check out the car for other drugs, and to make sure we were sober. David had texted a half-dozen times to check in, and I'd ignored every single one.

We got into the car, and I took the phone out.

All fine, busy day. Got sidetracked with some sightseeing your mom wanted to do. We will call in the morning.

He must have been sitting on top of the phone. My phone buzzed with a reply almost immediately: *Okay. Great. Hope you had fun. Glad Mom is safe. And you.*

And you. And you, he'd written. He was glad I was safe too. I frowned.

Kay clicked her buckle into place and cleared her throat.

"Okay, let's just drive as far as we can, try to make up some time."

"Sure," said Kay, subdued now. "David would have a fit if he knew we were driving this late at night."

"I know." I didn't like thinking about the fact that I'd just lied to him.

"He's anxious about the driving. It's his worst fear. He tried for months to get me to fly," she said.

I started the car, pulled out of the parking spot in front of the station and turned onto the road, trying to remember which way to the highway. "His worst fear? What, driving at night?"

"No, just ... someone he loves, driving, period. He hasn't owned a car in years. Well, five years, to be exact."

"Why? I mean, why no car? Why five years?"

Kay was silent for a minute, then sighed. "David got married when he was thirty-five," she started.

Oh. Married. Well, I guess that answers that, I thought to myself, imagining him in bed in Vancouver right this moment with his beautiful wife. "So, he's been married about … what, ten years?"

"Well, they were together for a few years before they got married," Kay replied, which didn't really answer it. "Melissa was great. Just one of those really fun, smart, calm people. If you had to imagine a person you'd want your child to grow up and marry, that was Melissa."

That *was* Melissa. My stomach tightened.

"After they'd been married about four years, she got pregnant. They had wanted to right away, but it took a while. David had to go away for work when she was seven months pregnant." She paused, took a deep breath, then continued. "She had an appointment with her obstetrician. David had gone to every single one with her up till then, but he was away for that one. He asked her to wait till he was home, but she just … well, she thought he was being over-protective to begin with, and she said no, she'd just go ahead on her own, it was fine, he worried too much."

"Kay—" I started. She was looking out the window at the darkness. It was so dark out here at night, with no cars behind or ahead of us on the highway.

"Well, anyway. She went to the appointment and everything was good, and she phoned to tell him from the parking lot … and then on the way home, someone ran a red light, and her car was …."

"I'm so sorry," I whispered.

"Yes, me too."

"Is David …." But I wasn't sure what I was asking.

"He does as well as he can."

I nodded, though Kay was looking away from me, and the car was too dark to see each other anyway. "Let's try to get to Fredericton; we have a reservation already, though we'll be very late," I suggested.

"If you get tired, let's just pull over and rest, okay?"

"Yes, sure," I answered. "Definitely."

8

WE WERE HALFWAY between Fredericton—we had managed to get to the hotel shortly after midnight—and Quebec City the next afternoon before Kay pulled out the list. I'd almost begun to hope she'd forgotten about it, in light of the police fiasco the day before. But no, there it was, in her front shirt pocket, neatly folded.

"All right," I said. "Let's see what we can cross off your list."

"Well, we stole something," she said, grabbing a pen from the glovebox and adding a checkmark next to #8. "You know, I didn't have 'get arrested,' but I should add it, since we were."

"We *weren't* arrested, thank God. I would have to tell David if we'd been arrested. We were just ... detained, sort of. Very minor."

"Number 21 ... get ... arrested," Kay intoned, as she added the words to the bottom of the list, then made a dramatic flourish of a checkmark next to it. "Oh, and #16: See the highest tide."

"But we didn't see the tide when it was in."

"No, but we were there. And we got the rock penis, and that's what counts." Kay waggled her eyebrows at me. It was becoming her signature look.

I sighed. "Okay, okay. If we're going to do all of those and come in anywhere close to your son's estimated journey time, we're going to have to get organized. What are some of the ones that are in Quebec or Ontario, and the ones that don't have any specific geographical location?"

Kay scanned the list. "Number 18: Buy something fun at a triple-X store. Okay, we could do that in Quebec City, since we're stopping there tonight."

"Buy something, like what?"

"I don't know; do you have anything battery-operated that needs replacing?"

"I don't own anything battery-operated, period."

Kay looked at me. "Are you joking?"

I blushed. "No, I'm not joking. I just ... I don't know. I was with Jack for a long time, and he didn't like 'weirdo things.' That's what he called them. Weirdo things. So no, I have no ... toys. Or whatever I'm supposed to call them."

Kay reached over and put her hand on my shoulder. "When's your birthday?"

"In April. The first—yes, like, April Fools' Day. Fitting, right?"

"All right, so that's ... seven months away. So we'll call it an early birthday present."

"Call *what* an early birthday present?"

"Whatever 'weirdo things' we find for you at the sex store."

"No. No, no, no. That's okay."

"I insist!"

"Kay, no."

"Don't you want to get all the items on our list finished?"

"Our list? That's not my list. That's *your* list."

"Your list now too, darling."

"Oh my God. Okay. Fine. We will go to a sex store in Quebec, and it won't be my fault if some perverted weirdo kidnaps us while we are there."

Kay looked at me for a moment, then began to laugh—it started small, but in short order she was howling, big whooping laughs, holding her hands to her stomach. "I'm not ... I'm not ... not laughing ... at you," she gasped out between laughs.

73

I looked away from the road for a second to glare at her, which only made her laugh harder.

"Oh God, Ruthie. Oh my God," she was gasping, trying to catch her breath and then breaking out into laughter again. "Oh jeez, I have to pee. I have to pee. Pull over!"

I looked at the empty highway behind me and pulled over onto the shoulder.

"Stop the car!" she yelled, still hiccupping and laughing. She yanked her door open before I'd come to a full stop and was hopping out as I pulled on the e-brake. She jogged over to the grassy ditch alongside the concrete, then looked up and down the highway.

"There's no one coming, just do it," I yelled out, not feeling particularly sympathetic. "I'm not looking." I turned my head away just as she appeared ready to yank her pants down.

"I can't believe I am doing this," she shouted, sounding embarrassed for once.

"Serves you right."

A minute later, she'd returned to the car. "Okay. Onward ho," she said, raising a fist in the air.

I turned the car on but just sat there.

"Let's go," Kay encouraged. "Hit the road. Let's boogie."

But I couldn't. Her teasing had opened something up, something I'd been avoiding thinking about. Kay reached out to poke me, but seeing my face, she paused. "What is it? Ruthie, what is it?"

I squeezed my eyes shut. "How come he didn't want to have sex with me, but he did with her?"

Kay didn't answer.

"I wanted to, a lot. I wanted to more than he did. He was always tired or coming to bed late. He'd even say he had a headache sometimes. A headache! Like a thing that some wife in a 1950s TV show says. But it wasn't the sex at all. It was me, obviously. Because he was having sex all the time with Flower Shop Girl, wasn't he? He still is."

I put my head down, letting my forehead rest on the steering wheel, and tried not to let myself cry. "I know I'm not … I'm not Flower Shop Girl. I'm not cute. And my boobs aren't … you know … I get it. I'm not that girl. But am I so awful? Why? What was wrong with me?"

Kay cleared her throat. "I'm sorry I teased you. I shouldn't have. This guy of yours, he wasn't a good match. He wasn't the right match. He didn't fit you. He did you a favour, in the end. You don't want to spend a lifetime mismatched. Trust me."

"I just—" I couldn't say anything else. My face felt hot and flushed, and I could feel an ugly-cry on the verge of breaking out of my mouth.

"Look, we'll skip the sex shop. We can skip it. I was just being silly."

I pressed my hands to my eyes, blocking out the light. Every few seconds, another car passed by, just a *whoosh* as it approached and then disappeared around the bend. People with places to go, with family waiting for them.

I shook my head, sniffed and took a deep breath. "No. We're going. We're going today. We're going to check into our hotel, and we're going to find the biggest goddamn sex store in the entire city, and you're going to buy some 'weirdo things,' and then we're going to go out and have dinner and a bottle of wine."

Kay nodded. "Okay, then. Let's do that."

I pushed my foot to the gas and pulled the car back out onto the highway. Two hours to Quebec City, and it felt like the West Coast was weeks away. At this rate, it would take all year.

9

WE WENT BY foot from the hotel to the sex shop, and I kept my eyes peeled for the telltale signs of what we were looking for—not that I had come across too many sex shops while growing up in small-town Quebec or living the last decade in small-town PEI. Small towns were not terribly conducive to such things; people mostly pretended sex didn't exist, except behind closed doors. But I'd seen enough movies and dicey cop dramas to know that these sorts of places always had neon-lit, hot-pink triple-X signs in the window, and a shady character or two hovering out front.

So I almost walked past the entire thing without realizing it because it was the exact opposite of what I'd decided it should look like. The sign above the door was a simple metal script, backlit with warm white light against blue paint, over two bay windows draped with velvet curtains.

Un Cadeaux d'Amour.

A gift of love. I wanted to roll my eyes. *Nice try,* I thought to myself, *more like a gift of freakiness.* But that was Jack talking, wasn't it? I waited on the sidewalk for Kay, who had been dawdling behind me and window shopping, to catch up.

"Here it is," I said.

She grinned. "Here it is, indeed. Well?" She waved her hand toward the entrance.

I shook my head. "After you. It's your idea."

She took the handle of the door and opened it. A small jingle rang out from a bell above the door frame, and a pretty, dark-haired Bettie Page look-alike smiled from behind the counter.

I steeled myself to make small talk, but she just nodded and went back to her work—which appeared to be the entirely normal, non-weird activity of running new receipt tape into the cash register.

Perfect. She wasn't going to ask me what I was looking for or try to sell me the Bang-o-rama 2000. I snorted out a laugh, surprising myself. Bang-o-rama 2000. Good one, Ruthie.

"All right, I'm going to wander," said Kay, looking around. There seemed to be two floors—the main one we were on now, then an open metal spiral staircase going to a loft.

The woman behind the counter saw us eyeing everything up from just inside the door, and she pointed to the back of the main floor. "Clothing, lingerie, jewelry and accessories on this floor," she said. Her arm swung upwards: "Most of the toys are on the second floor." Then she hooked a thumb over her shoulder. "Stairs to the basement are over there. All the fetish gear is downstairs," she smiled, her face the picture of calm innocence, as though she was behind the counter in a soda shop and had just told us that the cotton candy was upstairs, the burgers were on the main floor, and the milkshakes were stocked in the cellar.

"The basement. Fitting," Kay said with a smile.

The girl chuckled. "We call it the Dungeon."

My eyes went wide. Kay laughed. She was clearly far more at ease here than I was. It made me feel naïve and silly, but she hooked her arm around mine and pulled me along into the main part of the store.

"Well, then, want to shop together or on our own?"

"Um, yeah, I'll just browse on my own," I muttered.

The girl called over as we walked away from the front counter. "Chances are good whatever you're looking for is here. We're the biggest store in the city. If you can't find it here, we can get it for you—or it doesn't exist," she said.

"All right. Great. Thank you," I said, my voice low and tight.

She smiled again. "Have fun," she said, her voice entirely without judgment or teasing. In fact, it seemed to me that she was trying to make sure I felt comfortable—which was lovely, but it doubled my sense of being out of place. Even the store clerk could tell I was a dork.

I raised a hand halfway, in a gesture meant to indicate, "Okay, great, thanks, got it, we're good," and turned away. Kay had already begun to explore the main floor. I headed to the metal staircase.

"I'm going up," I said to Kay. When I reached the second floor, I scanned the entire space. No other shoppers. I looked over the railing to the main floor; Kay was busily working through a rack of lacy red things.

Good, no one to watch me. If I was going to look—really look—I wanted to do so unobserved. And I had to be methodical about it too. Scientific. I'd start on the left and look at everything along the shelving and walls, all the way to the back of the room, and then circle back around to the stairs. And at first glance, it seemed the best route: the stock had been laid out so that it started with small, simple things at the left of the stairs and, well, what appeared to be very large and rather complicated things to the right.

Simple and small was a good place to start, I thought. There was a huge diversity, by the look of things: some toys were smooth and sleek and modern, and one of those might have been a modern art sculpture, for all anyone would know if they saw it on your bedside table. Others were boxed in packages with porn stars on the outside, their contents specific and graphic—right down to the fine details. I was peering closely at the ridges and valleys on the side of a very lifelike, but rather large, dildo somewhere near the back of the store when I heard footfalls up the stairs.

I straightened quickly. "Hey, what's up," I said, the words coming out with a tone of forced casualness that was dripping with guilt, the way a teenager who has just been busted smoking a cigarette tries to sound. "Just, ah, checking things out back here. Interesting."

Kay smiled. "Found anything you want?"

"Me? Ha. No. I'm good. Anyway, I don't have a ton of spending money at the moment. I hadn't worked in ages before—" I stopped myself, realizing I was about to point out my lack of employment and income in recent months, which I'd mostly glossed over since we'd met. She already knew about Jack; she didn't need to know I'd spent several months wallowing in wine and bad movies, with a near-zero bank account. If she picked up on my comment, she didn't let on; she just carried on circling the room in the same route I'd taken.

"This is different," she said, and held up a banana-coloured item that looked like thick chopsticks that were attached at one end. She picked up the box under it, pulled on her reading glasses and let her head drop down to read the label. "For Kegel exercises. Good for sex and incontinence, apparently. I'm not sure I could use it for the sex, but I might need some help with the other thing before long."

"Yeah, well, didn't your list say 'have great sex'? So maybe you should be preparing, right?"

"The list didn't specify if the great sex was for me or you," she said. "Have you been doing your Kegels lately?"

I rolled my eyes dramatically, and she returned the item to its shelf and continued.

I wasn't enjoying being in the same area as Kay. I wanted to look closely at each item, see what it was and imagine how it might be used. To be honest, being in here was making me a bit … aroused. It had been a long time since I'd felt this way. So long that it seemed I'd almost forgotten what it was like. I could feel the memory of standing naked in front of Jack and Flower Shop Girl starting to rise up—I'd been worked up that day too, before I'd realized someone else was there. I closed my eyes. My face was flushed with the memory of the shame of it. Was getting horny going to trigger humiliation for the rest of my life?

"Stop," I whispered, to the ghost of Jack, to the ghost of myself, to no one in particular. "Stop. Now."

Kay must have caught my words, and she looked over at me. "All good, darling?"

I nodded. "I'm going to just go back downstairs. Don't rush."

I scurried down to the main floor. Lingerie seemed less risky—and less likely to trigger old memories. But when I got there, a young couple was already browsing. The woman was holding up a white nurse's outfit against the front of her body—a caricature of white vinyl and red accents—and the man was laughing but nodding.

I headed toward the stairs to the basement.

"Oh, Dungeon sale—10 percent off everything all week," the shop clerk said as I went past the counter toward the entrance.

"Great," I muttered, jogging down the stairs, noting as I went that there was, indeed, a sign above the stairwell that read: The Dungeon.

I entered a dark room with white spotlights highlighting four or five different areas around the room. What the hell: a mannequin was tied to a big, wooden X, her arms and legs attached with leather cuffs; in another spotlight, a wall of floggers and whips. I turned to my right and saw a series of leather straps with red balls, and I picked one up to take a closer look.

"Oh!" I jumped, as the phone in my back pocket began to buzz. Incoming call. David again.

I looked upward. *Really, God? This seems like a good time? Thank you very much.* I wasn't even entirely sure I believed in God, but it was reassuring to think someone was in charge of the cosmic mess of my life—including this phone call.

"Hello?" I said, putting the phone to my ear.

"Hi! Ruthie? It's me."

"David?" I asked, even though I knew it was. Like, what, I was trying to pretend that men with fabulously deep, sexy voices called me all the time, and I couldn't keep them straight?

"Yes. Yeah, just me. Just wanted to check in."

"Oh, we're in Quebec."

"The province or the city?"

"Both."

"Oh, I thought you'd be farther tonight."

I hesitated a moment. "Well, Kay seemed tired, from the driving. You know? So I didn't want to push it."

"Yeah, of course. You're the expert. I trust you."

Damn it, there it was again. He trusted me. He trusted me to be escorting his mother from PEI to Vancouver, not to be getting pulled over by cops and shopping for sex toys.

I realized he was waiting for a response, so I finally just said, "Thank you."

"Is she having fun, do you think?" he asked.

"Yeah, yes, I'd say she's having fun."

Speak of the devil: Kay came down the stairs just then, and her mouth went into an "oh" as she pointed at the mannequin on the wooden X.

"Saint Andrew's cross," she exclaimed, at the same moment that David asked another question.

"What?" I said into the phone.

"It's a Saint Andrew's cross. To tie people to," she repeated, louder, pointing toward it, assuming my question was for her.

"No, I meant David," I said, frantically shaking the phone in my hand and glaring at her.

"What did she say?" David asked into my ear. "Cross—"

"Oh, nothing. It's ... we're touring a church. Lots of history here. You know."

"A church!" Kay repeated, hooting with laughter.

"Is she okay?" David asked.

"David wants to know how you're doing," I said, pressing my lips into a thin line, eyes wide, feeling exasperated with both of them.

"Oh, I'm great," she said, moving closer. She leaned over toward the phone, so that she'd be heard clearly. "I got some souvenirs, hun," she said into the phone. She held up a trio of items she'd obviously picked up on the second floor.

"Oh that's great," David said into my ear. "She sounds like she's really enjoying herself." His voice was full of relief, as though he was smiling on the other end of the line.

"Yes, I think so. Okay, well, I should go; they don't really like people talking. During the tour. Of the church," I sputtered out.

"Oh sure, of course. I'll touch base tomorrow and—"

Kay leaned over again and pointed at the leather and red rubber item still in my hand. "That's a ball gag, darling. Not sure you're there yet, but maybe someday," she winked at me.

"What did she say? A ball—"

"David, have to go. Okay, bye. Thanks." I clicked off the phone and jammed it into my pocket, then slapped the leather item—the *ball gag*, according to Kay—back onto the shelf.

"Look, which do you like better: blue or realistic?" She held up two toys that she must have found on the top floor, one turquoise and the other a soft peach skin tone.

"Neither, Kay. I don't prefer *either* of them." I turned and stomped back up the stairs, circled around the front counter, ignored the Bettie Page look-alike when she asked if I needed some help, and stomped out onto the sidewalk—where I discovered it had begun to rain since we'd gone inside. "Fucking fantastic," I muttered.

Now I was angry *and* wet, without a jacket or umbrella, and I had no choice but to stand there and wait for Kay to join me. "It's a ball gag," I whispered in a high, sarcastic voice. I wanted to stomp, jump, bang my fists against the wall, have a temper tantrum and scream. Instead, I leaned back as close to the front window as I could, catching a bit of cover from the roofline above, and waited as my feet got wet.

Ten minutes later, Kay emerged with a huge bag and a smile.

"So, I—" she started.

"No. Don't talk to me." I was mad. I was cold and wet, and the phone call—along with Kay's glib teasing—had poked something in me. I felt foolish and silly: I was a full-grown woman, blushing my way through a sex shop, and Kay's teasing had made it all the worse. I glared at her, wanting to punish her even as I realized how childish it was.

"Okay, then," she said.

We walked in silence back to the hotel, and when we got to our floor, we turned in opposite directions—her room was to the left of the elevators and mine to the right.

"See you in the morning," I grumbled.

"See you in the morning," Kay replied. "Thank you, Ruthie."

I could tell by the tone of her voice that she was trying to be gentle, to acknowledge my mood, but I was too prickly to even respond. So I ignored her, unlocked my door and went inside, remembering as I bolted the lock behind me that I'd suggested on the drive here that we'd do a nice dinner and a bottle of wine after our shopping excursion. I could skip the dinner, but I wished I had the wine. Alone. Right now. That would make it tolerable, this awful aloneness in this strange place.

10

"I REALLY THINK we can just skip the family visit, can't we?"

Kay and I had made peace, somewhat, over a quiet but amicable breakfast of chocolate croissants and coffee at a shop up the street from the hotel. By the time I was fully caffeinated and buzzing on sugar, we had managed enough friendly small talk to be on mostly stable ground again.

But I was wishing I'd maintained a stony silence as Kay talked about staying overnight with my parents in Shawville. It was hard to be grumpy and stern when I was her friend again.

"No. We really can't. They're your parents. Trust me, they will want to see you."

"Oh, I have no doubt they will want to see *me*. I'm not entirely sure I want to see them," I replied.

I could see Kay eyeing me from the corner of my vision.

"Look, I love them. They're great. But they worry. They worry about me not being married, not having kids, not doing all the *stuff* I'm supposed to do. And it's always been like that. If my family was a village, then I'm the village idiot. I've always just … I don't know … messed things up."

"I wish I could say that parents always say and do the right thing, but I can tell you from experience on the other side that it's not true," said Kay.

I didn't have an answer to that, so I just stayed quiet. After a minute, Kay pulled her list out. "All right, #19—new hairdo.

How big is this town? Big enough for a decent hair salon?"

"Oh, yeah. Actually, my cousin owns an amazing place. She's great. People come from other towns to see her. Heck, when people move away, they wait for their annual visit back home to get their hair done."

"All right. Will you give her a call and see if there's a spot for me? Want to do something with yours too? It'll be my treat."

I glanced at myself in the rear-view mirror. I was looking a bit … shaggy. Not a bad idea, probably. "Okay. A trim."

"What? No highlights? No bright pink? Maybe a perm?"

I snorted. "I had a perm in Grade 7. Because, well, everyone had a perm in Grade 7. French poodle doesn't even properly sum it up. Seriously bad news."

"Okay, no perm. But … something?"

"A trim. Just a trim."

"All right, a trim it is. On me. When we pit stop next, call ahead and see if she can take us in the morning, maybe?"

"Are you doing this just to make sure that we have to sleep at my parents' house?"

"No. Yes. A little bit. Hey, free night, no hotel! Considering we're already behind schedule, I'm sure David will be happy with that."

I frowned at her. Thinking about David made my stomach drop. I was scared he'd discover what we had been up to, but even more, I was worried what he'd think of me for my part in it. I had gotten in the habit of checking and double-checking my phone, both hoping and dreading to see a text from him. Granted, this wasn't exactly what most people thought of when it came to "exciting texts"—it was mostly him checking in on his mother— but still, it was something new and, in its own small way, thrilling. In our last exchange, I'd said something funny, and when it garnered an LOL from him in return, I felt like I'd won the lottery. David struck me as someone who didn't laugh easily, or often.

"There. Let's stop for a snack," said Kay, pointing at an exit sign with the gas/food/rest symbols on it. "You can call then."

It was a bit early for a break, but why not. I could use another coffee and sugar boost. After our sex-shop argument, I hadn't slept very well. I'd been restless for hours, and though I'd chalked it up to the fight with Kay, the reality is that it was her son I was thinking about as I tossed back and forth in bed.

Her son—and all the "weird stuff" I'd seen in the store. Would he think it was weird? Or would he think it was maybe a little bit, sort of, fun?

✳

"For you, cuz, anything," said Kristen, my younger—and bubblier —cousin.

At age twenty-four, she'd opened her first salon. Three years later, she'd bought the town's one and only barbershop and managed to keep the old-timers happy by changing not too much— and bring in the younger generation by charging just enough. Both locations were hip and classic, cutting-edge and old school. She had staff, an accountant and more than one magazine write-up hailing her "big-city chops tucked away in small town-charm." In other words, she'd worked hard and done well. I was proud, and in a loving way, I was envious too.

"I've got a full set of appointments, but we'll make it work. A trim for you and a … what did you say? A colour for your friend? Done and done. Come in first thing; I'll open early so we can get you back on the road, and I'll have Denise lend a hand."

"Thank you so much; I really appreciate it. When I mentioned your place, Kay insisted we ought to go. You'll like her; she's great," I said.

"If she got you out of PEI and home for a visit, I love her already. I wish you could stay longer."

"I know. But I'm working, technically. Tick-tock on the clock, right?"

"Yeah. Maybe on the way back?"

I hesitated for a moment. The farther away I got from home, the less certain I felt about where I'd go after this. "Maybe."

Kristen knew better than to push. "See you tomorrow morning, then."

I turned off my phone, gave the screen a quick check to see if David had texted, and wandered back inside the restaurant. Kay was finishing a piece of pie.

"All right, appointment is set. I called Mom and Dad, too, and they're probably changing sheets in the spare room at this exact moment in anticipation of the brief return of the prodigal daughter and her wacky ward."

"Am I your ward? Am I wacky?" Kay squinted her eyes at me.

"You're a little of both, yes."

"You know, someday, when you're my age, you're going to have a moment where your offspring or some other younger person is going to imply that you are old or need help, and you will think back to this moment and feel really bad."

"If I live that long, I like to imagine that I won't feel bad about anything. I will have learned to be super Zen. I'll let shit go," I said, sniffing. I checked my phone again.

Kay laughed. "Good luck with that. Anything from my handsome son?"

"No. But I wasn't—"

"Sure."

"I don't have any—"

"I know. Of course. Entirely professional."

"He is very nice but not really my type, so—"

"Absolutely."

"Why do I feel like you're making fun of me?"

"Because I am, a little bit."

I stared at her. "Thanks."

"David is an oddball. I'm his mother; I'm allowed to say that.

He was before," she paused, *before the accident* going unspoken. "Even when he was a kid. Very routine, very rigid about things. Organized, detailed."

"That's probably a good thing, isn't it?"

"It is in some ways. Routine can be comforting. He has breakfast every Sunday at this little place in New Westminster—he gets up, gets on the SkyTrain and rides out the twenty minutes to this place, and I can pretty much guarantee that he orders three pancakes, two eggs sunny side up and two pieces of bacon. Every week. When Melissa was alive, she'd often have them going here and there on the weekends, doing different activities. After ... well, he started going again, every Sunday, same time, same meal. I think it was an anchor, you know? A thing to do, something to look forward to, when there was nothing else to do or look forward to."

I nodded, so she would know I was listening.

"We save ourselves, if we want to. If we can. People can survive awful things. I've survived a few myself. So have you."

"Oh," I said. "Jack and ... all that ... it's not like what David has had to deal with."

"No. But it was awful for you. It still is."

I looked down at my empty coffee cup. Was it awful? Was it *still* awful? "I used to be able to picture, exactly, the look on Jack's face when I ... you know ... walked out, and they were there. Sometimes I'd think about that look on his face for hours, trying to decide what it was. Shock? Anger? Comic surprise? I wanted it to be regret. But no matter how long I thought about his face, it never looked like regret."

Kay let me talk, not moving or even nodding.

"I can't picture his face now. I mean, in general I can; I know what he looks like. But that moment, which was so solid and precise, is sort of fuzzy now. I try to imagine that look on his face, and it's not clear to me anymore what it was. Maybe it wasn't even shock."

I thought about the last time I'd seen Jack face to face before I'd left. I'd arranged to meet him so I could hand off a few bits of paperwork for our apartment that I'd found among my things and that he might need—and part of me had wanted to see him one more time anyway. Maybe I hoped he'd look miserable or regretful or something. But he hadn't. He was happy. Like, really, really happy. Happier than I'd seen him in a long time. He wasn't rubbing it in my face. In fact, if anything, I could tell he was being subdued, conciliatory, allowing me to be rude and short and curt with him. But underneath it, he was relaxed, content. He looked … settled.

"I'm sure he didn't relish hurting you. Most people aren't that callous," said Kay.

"Yeah, well, he didn't try hard enough *not* to hurt me though, did he?"

"No, I suppose not."

"I wouldn't. Ever. If he liked someone else, or he just didn't love me anymore, there's a way to do that. An order. Finish one thing, start the next."

"Yes. Hypothetically speaking, that's the right way."

"No, it's not *hypothetical*. It just is," I insisted.

"People are complicated."

"Why do I always feel like you're on Jack's side when this comes up? You don't even know him."

"I'm not on his side. Just … devil's advocate, I guess. A habit garnered in a lifetime of unexpected outcomes. People are complicated; that's all I'm saying."

"I'm not. I'm not complicated at all. I wouldn't do what Jack did."

"Are you sure?"

"Yes." I stood up then, grabbing the bill and marching to the counter. If this continued, Kay and I were going to fight every inch of the Trans-Canada. And it was time to get back on the road. We had a few hours yet to get to my parents' home.

Kay stood nearby, scanning her list. I wanted to pull it out of her hands and rip it up. Thievery and sex toys and visits to old haunts. I just wanted to drive and get to David. Correction: I wanted to get *Kay* to David and be done with the entire thing. Finish the job and never see either of them again. It didn't feel as easy as I'd imagined it would be.

✳

"There's my girl!" My dad was waiting on the lawn as we pulled into the driveway. I'd given a rough estimate of when we'd arrive, but here we were, a few hours later than expected, and Dad was standing on the lawn like he'd known we were seconds away from pulling in. How had he known? Some sort of Dad-GPS-homing device? Considering how much I'd balked at coming here, it took me by surprise how happy I was to see him.

"Dad," I said, as I was pulled into his big bear hug.

It was the first time I'd been home since everything had fallen apart with Jack. They'd asked me a hundred times to come for a visit, but it had been easier to wallow—and drink, sleep all day and not shower—without anyone watching me and offering critique or advice.

Now that I was here, I couldn't remember exactly why I'd resisted.

"Baby girl, you look wonderful," Dad said.

I rolled my eyes and laughed. "Yeah, not sure about that; I've been driving for days and sleeping in hotels—but thank you all the same," I said.

"Your mom is at your sister's helping with ... I'm not sure ... something. A Halloween costume maybe? They'll all be over here for dinner. Kids too. They want to see their auntie."

I took a deep breath and smiled. "Great. That'll be ... great. Lots of noise."

"Yes," he laughed. "Too much noise."

Kay was stepping down out of the van then, and I turned to include her in the conversation.

"Dad, this is Kay—my *ward*," I said.

"If anyone needs *warding*, it's probably you," she said back, her tone crisp but full of humour. "Hello, Ruthie's dad. Thank you for having us."

"Any time. If we found out she'd been nearby and not come to say hello, we'd have considered disowning her," he said.

"That's exactly what I told her." Kay smiled. "See, I know a thing or two, Ruthie."

"Well, come in, and we can sit out back and catch up," Dad said, ushering us along. "Get the bags later; you've been driving all day."

With a happy sigh, I did as he instructed, following him through the front door, my eyes darting down the hall to my old childhood bedroom, to the photos along the wall, to the small kitchen that looked the same as it had for as long as I could remember, right down to the strawberry-dotted curtains in the window. "The best thing about home is that it never changes," I said, as we walked through the living room and out the sliding glass door.

"Well, it's changed a little," my dad replied, pointing to the corner of the deck.

"A hot tub? A hot tub. Seriously?"

"Yep. Your mom wanted one for years, so we finally put it in. We're in it almost every night—next summer I'll cover it with a little A-frame so we can sit under cover and use it even when it's snowing."

"Wow. It looks really great. I might have to check it out later," I said.

"You should. We love it."

I smiled at Dad. He sounded so excited and pleased with himself. Just then, my mom stepped out onto the deck.

"Yeah, he's bugging me to go for a tub every night," she said. As Dad went back inside, Mom leaned over toward me and, in a stage whisper, added: "I think he just likes the fact I'm only wearing a bathing suit. Easy access."

"Mom! Jesus, what a thing to say!"

"Says the girl taking the Lord's name in vain," she replied.

I snorted. Except for Christmas Eve and the occasional wedding or funeral, neither of us had been to church for at least twenty years.

Kay laughed. "Well, she's got a point, Ruthie. If you're already half undressed, things are just easier."

Kay and my mom laughed at that, as though they were old besties who had been making dirty jokes together for years.

"All right. Okay, enough. Hi, Mom," I said, leaning in for a hug.

"Hi, honey," she said, and squeezed me hard, all the things she wasn't saying about missing me and worrying over me translating through her arms around me and her hands stroking my back. "We're so glad you came."

"Me too," I said. And I meant it, more than I had expected to.

She pointed to the patio table, and we all took a seat as Dad returned with glasses and a pitcher of lemonade. It may have been September, but it felt like mid-August: dry and hot.

"Well, I got Andy's dog costume finished up," Mom said, referring to the second of Becky's children. "Now we need to find a crown and a magic wand to go with Allie's mermaid outfit."

"Crown and wand?" I asked.

"Apparently she wants to be a mermaid-witch queen—but a good one, not a bad one. She's five," she continued, explaining to Kay. "By the time Halloween arrives, she'll have probably decided she wants to be a horse policewoman or a librarian from outer space. This was a lot easier when you guys were little. We just put some makeup on your faces, and off you went in your dad's old shirts or whatever was around."

"Yeah, it's gotten a bit more upscale, I guess," I said.

"A lot more upscale," my mom added.

We sat in silence for a bit, enjoying the lemonade and the rest.

Dad and Kay got started talking about her time in Ottawa before David was born, and though I tried to listen in, my brain was tired from being behind the wheel, and I felt myself zoning out.

When my sister arrived with her four kids, it was like an explosion into the backyard: noise and movement everywhere at once. The kids came rushing around me, hugs and kisses and "I love yous" pouring out of them. I hadn't seen them since last Christmas. It was reassuring to discover that not even the youngest one was shy to see me again. I couldn't believe how much bigger they all were, and I told them so over and over, much to their delight.

They talked over each other to tell me about birthday parties and teachers and friends at school and hockey lessons, and I tried as hard as I could to listen and nod and say, "Oh, that's great," at the right time, and eventually the barrage died down and they wandered over to the swing set on the far side of the yard.

This was the hardest part about not living here: missing out on my nieces' and nephews' everyday lives. "I miss them," I said, feeling wistful.

Becky leaned over to hug me. "They miss you too. Maybe you should come back and stay?" She said it with a joking tone, but underneath I knew she was testing the water.

"Maybe," I said. For the first time in a long time, the idea was almost appealing.

My mom called out from the kitchen for extra hands to carry food out to the table. Kay and I stood up, but Dad shushed us and told us to sit back down and relax. He didn't have to tell me twice: I was dead on my feet all of a sudden, the accumulated exhaustion and emotion from the last few days suddenly catching up to me. I'd get to bed early tonight, I told myself, as bowls of macaroni and potato salad landed in front of me. Dad said the burgers would be one more minute on the BBQ, and then we'd eat. I sat back and let everyone else bustle around me.

Kay looked at me, her eyes narrowing. "You look tired."

"I am."

"Maybe we ought to stay two nights? Just catch up a little. Rest."

"Hmm. Maybe. We'll see. We have the hair appointments in the morning, so that will take a chunk of time out of our driving schedule anyway."

"And I want to go to Sand Bay, don't forget."

I had forgotten, actually. Damn. That alone would eat up another couple of hours, and we'd have to double back through Shawville to get onto the main route through Ontario anyway. "Yeah, maybe two nights, then," I said. "We can figure it out tomorrow."

"I'll call David after dinner and let him know."

I wanted to debate it with her, but I was so tired that I didn't have the energy to, so I just nodded. As everyone sat down and loaded plates with food, I sat back in my chair and closed my eyes, listening to the kids fight over who deserved the biggest cob of corn.

It was good to be here. People who loved me had been in short supply lately, and here was a full table of them. I felt for the phone in my pocket. It hadn't buzzed all day. I couldn't help but wonder what David was doing just then, and whether he liked macaroni salad and corn on the cob and loud children.

Not that it made any difference to me.

11

WE SAT AROUND the table for ages after dinner was over, enjoying the cooling temperatures as the sun began to set. The kids wrestled and fought, played games, climbed the swing set, tried to teach my parents' dog how to sit and roll over. The massive Saint Bernard, who was at least twelve years old, just looked at them grumpily and lay down, so they settled for stroking his head and discussing if he was older than Grandpa in dog years or younger.

"He's definitely younger," I shouted over to them. "No one is as old as Grandpa." The joke was aimed at my dad, of course, but the kids got a laugh out of it too.

"It's lovely, isn't it," I said to my sister. "They're getting to that age where they get grown-up humour. It's not just endless knock-knock jokes that don't even make sense."

"Yeah, it is … but they're also getting to that age where they want things like iPhones and tablets," she said. "And once the oldest has something, it seems like it's not long before it trickles down the line."

"And you're a total softie pushover who can't say no," said my mom.

"Well, that's true," said Becky.

Just then her youngest came running up to the deck. "Another popsicle, please," she said, her eyes imploring, the 'please' dragged out in that way that only seven-year-old kids can really do just right.

"Oh, all right. Get one for everyone," her mom answered. Maisie scampered off to the freezer in the garage, and I raised my eyebrows at my sister.

"See? Total pushover, sis," I said.

"Hey, you'd be worse than me!"

"Good thing I don't seem to be the baby-making sort, then," I said. "Or the marrying sort, I guess."

She laughed. I could tell that she felt relieved at my ability to make jokes about myself in this way. I tried to recall the last time we'd talked on the phone. I was sure I had answered every question with one-word responses and hung up as quickly as I could.

"Oh, I think you're the marrying sort, deep down," said my dad. "Just need to find the right one to marry."

"Don't worry about marriage. Living in sin is just fine," said my mom. "So long as there's lots of sin going on."

Everyone fell silent, and then we all burst out laughing. My mom still surprised me every once in a while with an unexpected bit of immodesty under her prim and proper exterior.

"Yeah, well, I'm not so sure living in sin worked out very well for me," I said. I looked over at the kids playing in the darkening yard. "Jack was the one who always said he wasn't much for the idea of marriage, whenever it came up. Just a piece of paper and all that. And I just … went along with it, I guess. Sin by default? But maybe next time, hey?" I looked around with what I hoped was an optimistic smile, trying to lighten the mood again. But everyone was frowning—except Kay, who at that moment seemed to be as perplexed as I was about the mood at the table. "What? I was just joking around."

My dad grimaced, like he'd sat down on something sharp in the middle of a very quiet library and didn't want to yelp out loud. My mom was inspecting her hands as if she'd never seen them before, and my sister was pushing icing from her carrot cake around on her plate. No one was looking at me. Except Kay. Later

I would think that it seemed Kay had figured it all out before anyone even spoke, the way she looked at me like she was both sad and sympathetic but also steely too—like she was trying to lend me some strength before I even knew I would need it.

"What?" I forced a laugh. "What is it?"

My sister finally looked up.

"Ruthie, it's—"

"What. What is it? Tell me."

"It's Jack," she said, voice flat.

"What do you mean—what's Jack?"

"He's ... well, he's getting married, Ruthie."

One of the kids yelled out, drawing the others over to an anthill in the corner of the yard. The noise made me jump. "No, I don't think that's—" I started, but my sister cut me off.

"He is. He phoned Steve two weeks ago and told him. Steve told us." Steve was Becky's brother-in-law, her husband's oldest brother. It was technically through Steve that Jack and I had met in the first place. Steve had been the best man at Becky and Adam's wedding, and I had been the maid of honor. Jack had come into town unexpectedly, returning home from an overseas backpacking trip, and he was staying with Steve the week of the wedding. They were best friends going back to childhood. Becky and Adam had suggested finding him a suit and tie and inviting him along to the big day—and Jack and I had spent most of the night dancing with each other.

"When?" I asked, my voice flat.

"Now. This week. They went to Hawaii. Just with family and a few friends. Steve is there."

I could feel my jaw locking on itself, my lips tight over my teeth, the rest of my face blank as a hot rush roared through me. All of the rage that had slowly eased away came roaring back, as though it had only been hidden these last few weeks—it was as big and awful and dark as it had ever been. Hawaii. I'd suggested

CHRISTINA MYERS

going there a dozen times, a hundred times, and he'd always said it didn't interest him. He'd always said getting married didn't interest him either.

But Hawaii and marriage were just fine, it turned out. I pushed my chair back and stood up. I wanted to scream—not just to scream, but to howl and beg and sob and carry on until someone, Jack maybe, would tell me *why*. Why I was so easily lost, why having me meant so little. Why replacing me had been so easy.

Most of all, I wanted to know why he hadn't told me years ago and let me go my own way before I'd begun to assume that the rest of my life was really the rest of *our* lives. Together. Sympatico. Conjoined.

I closed my eyes tight. It wasn't rage at all. It was sorrow, really—and not even, I realized for the first time, sorrow over Jack, or even for myself. It was sorrow for a life I thought existed; a life that had unravelled years before it came apart, a life that deep down I'd known wasn't right for me.

Everyone looked at me, hesitant, bracing for a storm, but the storm had already passed. Or perhaps I was simply standing in the eye of it—everything inside me was flat, suddenly. I'd spent six months grieving a life that I only just now was realizing hadn't been the right one for me anyway.

"I'm going to bed. Mom, can you please show Kay where the second room is? Kay, we have to be at Mint for our hair appointments at 8:00 a.m., so we will be leaving at 7:30." No one said a word. Kay made eye contact, frowned and nodded.

I walked through the house like I was a ghost gliding above the floor: I was moving, but everything in me was still and calm. When I got to my old room, I saw that my dad—my gentle, sweet, kind dad—had gotten our bags out of the car, and mine were sitting on the foot of my bed.

I moved them to the floor, and I lay down on top of the old hand-stitched quilt that had been on this bed for as long as I could

98

remember. I let my fingers run along the stitching at the edges of each quilt square, tracing the block and then each of the smaller pieces inside. *Wedding ring*, I thought to myself. This pattern was known as a wedding ring quilt. Often given as a gift to newlyweds, my grandmother had told me—this one had been a gift to her, in fact, on her wedding day. I'd grown up sleeping under this quilt, thinking about how someone might someday give me a blanket like this to wish me well on a big day.

I curled onto my side and shut my eyes. "Just sleep," I whispered to myself. "Just go to sleep."

12

I WAS GROGGY and grumpy when we got to Mint the next morning. Overnight, summer had disappeared, and fall had arrived: there was a chilly dew over everything, and the air was cold in my lungs. I liked autumn well enough, but I was tired and achy from a long night of tossing and turning, and somehow the cooler weather was adding insult to injury.

Kay and I had packed our bags back into the van and said our early-morning goodbyes to my parents, with the idea that after our haircuts, we'd get right on the road rather than double back home. We'd parked right out front, and as we approached the front door, I could see Kay scanning up and down the street.

It *was* a pretty view: a classic Norman Rockwell main street, stores not yet open, a few early orange and yellow leaves skittering along the edge of the street. It made me miss living here. Home always feels like a comfort, even if you don't want to stay. I pulled the salon door open and let Kay enter ahead of me. Inside it was warm, full of soft lighting and the smell of brewing coffee.

"Hi!" My cousin popped out from the back room, all smiles and blonde cheerfulness. She exuded happiness, the kind of person you wanted to stay close to in hopes of picking up some of the sunshine she radiated. She hugged me tight, then turned to Kay. "This must be Kay?"

"Yep. Kay, this is Kristen; Kristen, this is Kay."

"So you're stuck with this cousin of mine from one side of the country to the other, eh?" Kristen asked. "Is there hazard pay for that?"

"Very funny," I said. "If anyone deserves hazard pay here, it's me. You wouldn't believe the things this one wants me to do." I nodded my head in Kay's direction, but she just chuckled.

"Hey, if you must go on a journey, might as well make it an adventure," she said.

The bell over the door jingled, and Kristen's second-in-command, Denise, came in. "I'm here! I'm here! I'm not late!"

"You're a little bit late," Kristen replied.

"But you love me, so you won't fire me today."

"I won't fire you today. No promises tomorrow."

I had a feeling this conversation was played out several times a week, and the jab and jostle of their back-and-forth made me miss Jules desperately. Maybe I'd call her tonight from the hotel. Or text. Or email. Yes, that was safest. Email.

"Okay, ladies, into the chairs," said Kristen, gesturing toward the two closest seats. "What exactly are we doing today? We have some time—we don't even open for a couple of hours, and I shuffled the first appointments. So we can go a little crazy. Kay?"

I'd never seen Kay look hesitant or shy, but she did just then. "Well, I guess I was thinking ... I mean, on a scale of one to ten, how crazy would it look if I did some colour?" she asked.

"Oh, not crazy at all! We have lots of women who cover up their grey every month with blonde, brunette, whatever you like."

"Well, I was thinking more like ... a bright colour. Like pink or blue ... or purple," she said.

Kristen's eyes lit up. "Oh, yes. Yes yes yes. I have an idea. Do you trust me?"

"Sure," said Kay, beaming. "Do as you will!"

Kristen rubbed her hands together, gleeful, then looked at me. "Ruthie? Colour for you too?" she asked hopefully.

I laughed. "No. No way."

As I'd tossed and turned all night, I'd had this idea of chopping it all off—going full Sinéad O'Connor—but it was a cliché thing to do: didn't every heartbroken girl in every movie chop her hair off in the wake of being left by some guy? "How about just a trim."

"A trim and highlights."

"Umm …."

"A big trim and lots of highlights it is!" Kristen turned to Denise and indicated that she'd cover Kay while Denise could start on me. "Okay, ladies, let's do it."

❋

"Holy shit," I whispered. "Holy shit, Kay. That's …."

"Isn't it?" She twirled around in front of me, fluffing her hair out with her hands.

I'd spent most of the last few hours with my eyes closed, fighting off a headache from lack of sleep. Without my glasses, I couldn't see much more than a fuzzy shape a few feet away that I knew was Kay because I could hear her chatting away to Kristen. My trim and highlights had taken less time, and I'd gone out to the van to rearrange a few things. By the time I'd come back inside, Kay was done, and Kristen and Denise were beaming.

She looked amazing. Her salt-and-pepper hair was equal parts glossy silver and deep indigo, and it had been flat-ironed even straighter than it normally was. The silver was on top, with the indigo on the underlayer—it peeked out when she moved, and as she twirled, it seemed like the silver and indigo were intermixed.

Kay was ecstatic. "I know I should be too old to let a new hairdo make me feel so good, but God, it does. I might even not be grumpy about moving to BC for the rest of the day."

I laughed. "Whatever works." I was pretty pleased with my hair too. It was trimmed up to my shoulders and looked healthier than it had in ages. The highlights were modest—just strands of gold here and there among my natural colour. Denise had given the ends a bit of a curl, and it looked "done"—like I'd taken the time and effort to do something with it, rather than just wash and go, which had become my usual over the last several months. "Well, we're a fine pair of hotties, I think," I said, grinning back at her. "Told you this place was good."

"Better than good," said Kay. "Okay, we'd best get going. Big day today."

We were going up to Sand Bay first, for whatever mystery location Kay needed to visit, and then we had a long drive after that to our planned overnight stop.

"Thank you, ladies; you have made my day and possibly my year," Kay said.

Kristen hugged me, tight, and then Kay. "Be safe."

"We will. Always." I replied.

"Except for the mechanical bull. We still have to ride a mechanical bull," Kay said to me. "Number 23 on the list."

"I don't remember a mechanical bull on the list. And the list only went to #20, until you added #21—get arrested. There is no #23. You're making that up," I said.

Kristen laughed. "What's this?"

"Long story," I said, and looked at Kay. "No mechanical bulls."

"We'll see," she replied, then turned and left the store.

"See you, cuz," I said, as I hugged Kristen one more time and followed behind Kay. We climbed into the van, and I started the engine.

"All right," said Kay. "Let's go to Sand Bay." She squared her shoulders and put her head back, steeling herself for the day ahead. Whatever was in Sand Bay, I had a feeling it wasn't going to be as fun as a huge penis rock.

13

"HERE. IT'S HERE. Turn in."

We'd been driving in silence for an hour, the route from town to Sand Bay quiet and easy. Once Kay had realized I knew exactly where I was going, she let me drive and spent the time staring out her window. When we came around a corner with a particularly large maple, Kay had looked up at it, then sat forward.

"I remember this tree," she'd said, and a moment later, she told me where to turn in.

I'd driven this road before. It went up toward the lake, about a kilometre in, with smaller branches of road stemming off of it, and at the lake's edge it turned north and circled along the shore. The area was full of hundreds of cottages, tucked away in the woods and scattered along the lake's edge. "How long since you've been here?"

"More than … forty years, I guess. Forty-six years. I was last here in August, forty-six years ago."

"Is the place still here?"

"I have no idea. I hope so. Just stay on the main route, and when it comes along the lake drive, there's a small road that goes opposite the main; take that."

I didn't recall there being another road where she was talking about, but I nodded. This was her idea, and if we couldn't find it, then at least we'd tried. The minivan bumped and jostled over the smooth dirt road, gravel spitting up behind us as we drove in a swirl of dust. Kay pointed ahead of us.

"So beautiful, isn't it?"

We were headed into a section of lane covered by a canopy of red and orange and yellow leaves. A light breeze skittered the fallen leaves across the road, and I knew, even with the windows closed, there'd be a nip in the air. I'd spent enough time in this area to have learned that summers run hot and long, but one day, usually in October but sometimes as early as Labour Day weekend, everything suddenly shifted, and from then on it was coats for morning walks and toques in the evening.

It had not occurred to me to worry about winter when we'd set out from home, but now I couldn't help but wonder if we would hit snow when we crossed the prairies—or worse, the mountains. We had to pick up the pace, list or no list. "Turn off here," said Kay.

I was surprised to realize there was indeed another lane exactly where she'd said there would be. I had driven past here many times on the way to my aunt's cottage farther up the main road, but I'd never really noticed this narrow side path, its entrance crowded with brush.

"Okay, this one," she said, finally, noting a smaller-yet path off the road itself, tucked in between large trees whose branches hung so low that I almost instinctively ducked my head as we drove underneath.

It opened on the other side to a long driveway, nothing more than two tracks in the grass, really, that led all the way down to a concrete boat launch at the water's edge. A small cottage—the kind that looks like it's had various additions built over the years, a room here, an entryway there—was to the left. The dock was still out, which led me to believe that people were still using this cottage; if they had closed up for the season, they'd have pulled the dock in to store it for the winter.

"Are we allowed to be here? Do you know the owners, Kay?" She didn't answer.

I stopped the car, angling off slightly in case someone came in behind me, but not pulling in so far in that it was fully trespassing. As though I might in fact just be a wayward traveller who had pulled off to double-check some instructions or a map.

"Do you know the owners?" I asked again. Kay was silent. I looked over at her. She was sitting entirely still, her eyes scanning the house, the dock and the lake. Finally, she took a deep breath.

"I used to come here sometimes. With a friend. He owned it, then. He was …," she let the sentence die off. "It was a long time ago. I just want to … see." She unbuckled her belt, reached over and opened the door, and quietly slid out of the car, slamming the door behind her.

"Shit," I whispered under my breath, and then I opened my door and got out too. She was halfway to the dock already, passing right by the cottage itself. "Kay," I said, in a stage whisper. "This is …."

This is what, exactly? Illegal? Weird? There were no other cars in the drive, but what if someone pulled in and demanded to know why we were wandering around their property? I'd just assumed that Kay knew someone here, but now that we'd arrived, I wasn't sure what was going on.

"Kay," I said again, louder. She didn't pause at all, or even turn her head. I stood at the car door, watching. She went straight to the dock and walked all the way to the end. And then she just stood there. Looking out.

A minute passed—which felt like ten minutes—and still she hadn't moved. She was too far off now to call her name without screaming it, so I waited. There was a movement in one of the windows at the side of the cottage. The side screen door opened, and a young woman stepped out. She looked toward Kay, then back at me. I put a hand up in greeting.

Shit. I started walking toward her. If Kay had heard the noise of the screen door swinging open, she'd ignored it. She was standing still as stone.

The woman looked toward Kay and back to me, the look on her face friendly but uncertain.

"Can I help you? Are you … lost?" She looked back at Kay again.

"Oh, I'm sorry. I'm Ruth." I put my hand out. She shook it, but the questioning look on her face remained. "Um, no, not lost. I'm … she's … well, we were in the area. I grew up in Shawville."

Hearing I was a local worked its magic. Just like that, I was safe. Her stance relaxed. "Oh, okay," she said, smiling. "We come down from Ottawa, but we always try to get to the fall fair in Shawville. It's great."

"Yeah, it's awesome," I said, smiling back. "My sister was fall fair queen, like, four years in a row."

She chuckled. "A very big deal, I'm sure."

"Oh, you have no idea. She still talks about it."

"So, um, is there something I can help with?" she asked again. "Is she okay?"

"Oh, yes, yes. No, she's fine. It's just that we were coming through this area, and she's moving out to Vancouver and … well, she asked if we could come by here. Apparently she used to come up here years ago with a friend. I don't really know." I gestured toward Kay. "I'll go get her; she's just … in dreamland, I guess. It's beautiful here," I said, trying to suggest it was the landscape that had mesmerized Kay.

"She used to come here? To this house? Weird," she said.

"Yeah, that's what she said."

"My dad's uncle built this place way before I was born, and it's always been in our family. Who did she say she came with?"

"I don't know. She said a friend. But it was years ago; she said she hadn't been here in, like, forty years."

"Well, the only people up here then would have been my Uncle Bernie and his wife. That's my great-uncle, my dad's uncle, the one who built it. She must have come up with Sophia, maybe, but … I don't know much about her. She died a long time ago, and Bernie has been in BC for thirty years now."

I shrugged. "I don't know. She just asked to come up. I'm really sorry; we didn't mean to trespass," I said.

"No worries."

We stood and watched Kay for a moment, and then—like someone had flicked a switch and turned her back on—Kay turned and walked back up the dock toward us. She'd been crying. I could see that her eyes were glassy and wet, and her cheeks were damp.

"Hi. I'm so sorry," she said, trying for a smile. "We didn't realize anyone was home, and I just wanted to … look."

The woman smiled, a gentle smile. "You used to come up here?"

"Yes, a long time ago. I just always had such good memories of it—I guess I wanted to see the view one more time," she said. "A lot of memories," she added, her eyes scanning the property.

"You must have known my great-uncle and great-aunt, then," the woman said. "Bernie and Sophia?"

Kay's eyes widened, but she didn't answer.

"Bernie and Sophia Kowalski?" the woman asked again.

Kay nodded. I could see her swallow and then plaster a small half smile on her face. "Yes, I knew them."

"I never met Sophia," the woman said. "She passed away before I was born. But I just saw Uncle Bernie last summer; we did a road trip to Vancouver and stopped in to visit him."

"Oh," said Kay. She opened her mouth, then closed it again.

Now I was curious and jumped in. "He lives out there? In Vancouver?"

"No," she answered. "In Rossland; it's actually closer to the Alberta border than Vancouver, but we passed through there. Really beautiful area, actually."

"Is he … still …," Kay stammered.

"Alive? Yes, he's doing great. He's been there for years and years. Since before I was born. After his wife passed away, he went out there, and he just never came back," she said. There was a pause in the conversation then, as we all just looked at each other.

"Well, I'd better get back inside; my daughter is napping. No rush, feel free to look around more, if you want."

"Oh, thank you, but we'll get back on the road, I think," Kay answered. She blinked a few times, and then suddenly she looked herself again and smiled at the woman. "Thank you for not calling the police on a daft old lady for sneaking onto your dock."

The woman laughed. "Any time." She wandered back to the house, and the screen door creaked open, then slammed behind her.

I looked at Kay. "So …."

"Let's go."

"No, I mean … so, are you going to tell me what's going on here?" I continued.

"No, I'm not. Let's go."

"Kay …."

But she'd walked to her side of the van and was already climbing in, pulling the door shut behind her. I followed suit, buckled up and turned on the engine.

"Kay," I said.

She was looking out the window. "Let's just go."

I put the car in reverse, backed up and turned so I could head back out the way we'd come. In the rear-view mirror, I could see the dock and then the cottage disappearing behind the curtain of leaves and low branches, and I looked over at Kay.

She was staring down into her lap, her list out, pen ready to check off another item. If she had the urge to look back, she didn't indulge it, but tucked the list back into her pocket and stared straight ahead.

14

WE REJOINED THE Trans-Canada Highway south of the Ottawa River in Ontario and headed west. The real, actual west, someplace past the prairies, felt so far away it was hard to imagine it. I knew that David had Sudbury on his list of "suggested" stopovers, so I suggested to Kay that we ought to try to get that far. It would be about four and a half hours, via North Bay, from Sand Bay; it would have been an easy day, if we had not spent a few hours getting our hair done and made another side stop at the cottage. Still, Kay said she was up for it, so I set my mind to the task of driving and tried not to think about anything else. Which lasted about three minutes.

"So who are Bernie and Sophia?"

Kay glanced in my direction, then looked back out her window, her hand gesturing in a dismissive way.

"You knew them, though," I urged.

"Yes. Well, I knew Bernie."

She doesn't want to talk about this, I thought to myself. Which made me want to talk about it more.

"We'll need to make a pit stop soon—can you pull in at the next rest stop?" Kay asked.

"Sure," I replied.

"Your parents are really lovely," she said.

"They are, yes."

"And your sister too."

"Yes, she's great." I knew exactly where she was going to go next.

"How are you feeling about the news?" she asked. "About Jack."

"Mostly trying not to think about it, actually," I replied. "Thanks for the reminder."

Kay leaned her head toward me silently, a sort of wordless apology, then sighed. "All right. I was in love with Bernie, and I think it is safe to say that he was in love with me. We lived in the same building in Ottawa, and we fell in love, and we'd come up here to the cottage. It was his; no one else used it then. He owned it, he built it. We'd come up for the weekend, and I'd help—you know, hold a piece of wood while he hammered it in place, paint a wall, that sort of thing."

I tried to imagine Kay as a young woman, disappearing into the woods with her boyfriend. Her photos at home were all of her husband, Bill, and of David. Mostly David, at soccer games and school events and the like. There were so few photos of Kay that it was hard to shape the image of her in any other form than the one sitting next to me.

"That must have been a bit scandalous. An unmarried couple spending the weekend together unchaperoned. That was kind of a big deal then," I said.

Kay turned and looked out her window. "You have no idea."

"Did you ever wish you'd married him?"

"If he'd asked, if we'd been able to, I would have. But ...."

"But what?"

"It's a long story."

"We have time," I urged.

"It's complicated."

"That's okay. We have time."

"Ruthie. That's code for 'I don't want to talk about it,'" she said, her voice edging into tightness.

I held my tongue for a moment, then asked: "Do you think about seeing him again?" I glanced over at her, letting my eyes leave the road for a split second. She was staring at me, her eyes wide and sad.

"Every day. But it's too late now. Too much time has passed. And I'm too old," she said, shrugging.

My phone, plugged into the charger and sitting in the console, trilled out a noise.

"Text message," I said. "Probably David; no one else is talking to me except my parents, and they don't really use this newfangled technology."

"I don't blame them," Kay laughed. "Here, rest stop, twelve hundred metres. Let's pull in. You can check the message, and I'll use the bathroom."

I nodded, and when the exit yawned its way off the main road, I eased the van onto it, following the curve around.

15

WE PULLED INTO Sudbury after seven and spent a half-hour going in circles, looking for the hotel I'd called earlier in the day for a reservation. By the time we arrived, we were hungry, our nerves frayed and our bodies sore and tired. We got the key cards for our rooms—joined by a door but one room for each of us—and dragged our suitcases to the elevator.

"Let's just do room service, yes?" I asked.

"Great plan. Eat. Shower. Bed," said Kay.

I sighed. Perfect. I didn't want to talk, think or do anything other than watch old *Magnum PI* episodes on the TV while eating an overpriced BLT and fries, or some other equally bland hotel room-service meal. We went in our separate doors, then I opened the door between our rooms a crack and stuck my head through.

"I'm going to order some food, then jump in the shower before it arrives. Want me to order you something?" I asked her.

"Soup, whatever kind of soup there is. That would be good. And some toast."

I nodded, then dug around on the desk until I found the hotel information binder and flipped to the room-service menu. It was easy enough to settle on a meal for myself with the limited options, and I called down to place the order, adding a soup of the day and toast for Kay.

"Okay, the order's in," I shouted through the crack in the door. "About a half-hour, they said. I'm going to shower."

I locked the bathroom door behind me and had just started to undress when my phone rang. I dropped my shirt and grabbed the phone.

"Hello?" I said.

"Ruth." It was David—sounding more serious than usual, which was a feat, considering his base level.

"Everything okay?" I asked.

"Yes, I was going to ask you the same," he said. "I worried all afternoon, when you texted that you were on the way to Sudbury. That's a tough stretch of highway and a lot of big trucks, and … well, anyway, I just wanted to make sure you were both safe and sound."

I looked at myself in the mirror, half nude, and covered my breasts with my free arm. "Yes, safe and sound. We just checked in, and dinner is on its way. I think it'll be an early night; we're both tired."

"Just about dinner time here, too," he said. "What's that noise? In the background?"

"Oh, the shower. I was just about to … I started the shower; I was going to have a shower before dinner came, so it's just running. I'm not *in* it, just … I was just getting ready to get in it, and yeah, that's the noise."

"Oh," he said, a slight jump of surprise in his voice. "I should let you go then. Don't want to waste all of Sudbury's water."

I could tell he was smiling, and it made me smile back. "Good point. Okay, well …."

"I'll be just hanging around, if you wanted to text me after. I mean, to let me know how Mom is doing. If you want."

I grinned. "Yes, I'll send you a message after we eat. And I'll let Kay know you called."

"Thanks, Ruth."

"No problem."

"Okay, have a good shower. I mean, you know, a good dinner. Have a good night. And I'll talk to you after. Maybe."

"Okay."

"Bye."

"Bye."

"Bye," he said again.

I laughed.

"Okay, bye for real," he said. The line was still live for another few seconds—I could hear him breathing and knew he had not yet disconnected—and then finally the echo in my ear went blank, and I looked at the screen. Call ended.

I let my arm fall away from my chest and looked at my body in the mirror, thinking of *that* day, another shower, another bathroom, stepping out to find Jack there. I set the phone down, put my new hair up into a shower cap and stepped into the hot water.

❋

I woke up just before 8:00 a.m. and rolled over to grab my phone, opening the text thread with David and typing out a quick message: *So sorry, I fell asleep on top of the blankets with my dinner half eaten. I meant to message you.*

Shit. He'd asked me to get a hold of him after we'd eaten, and it was more a friendly suggestion than a boss-employee request. But I'd finished in the shower just as the room-service knock came, then thrown on a T-shirt and shorts to answer it, and fifteen minutes later I was asleep on one side of the bed, with a tray of half-eaten grilled cheese sandwich and Caesar salad on the other side. The bedside light was still on, and somehow I'd slept through without any covers on and the stinky garlic of the salad next to my head.

His reply was quick: *No problem. You must have been tired*

I guess so. I didn't feel it but I crashed hard

My mom is exhausting lol

No lol! She's great, and fun

And exhausting

Okay, a little, sometimes. But the driving is too, I guess

Yeah

Did you have a good sleep?

I paused, feeling like I'd suddenly crossed a line. Asking if he had a good sleep is very *personal*, like asking if he had a good time being half-naked in his bed. Or completely naked, for all I knew. There was a thought. Naked David.

No, I tossed and turned. Been awake an hour already and it's not even dawn yet

Oh. Sorry

I'm used to it. I don't sleep well. Coffee will be on IV this morning lol.

He's funny, like this, in words, on a screen.

Do you think tonight we could maybe Skype?

Oh God. Talk by video? Like … what, just visit with each other? Like, a date?

I wanted to see my mom

Oh.

Of course. To see his mom.

And say hi, to you

Yes, of course. Not sure where we will stop yet

Okay, we can figure it out later

Okay

Ruth?

Yes?

I'm really glad we found you

We. Right. I was here for his mother, not for him.

Me too

Yes? Not ready to quit yet? lol

Only a few times a day

Oh really????

I'm kidding. A few times by noon

Lol

I'd better get up. Might have a swim before your mom wakes up, then get on the road early

You have a lot of prairie ahead of you

Yes but not yet

The phone stayed silent for a long time, and I wondered if his desk phone had rung and taken him away or if he was staring at his screen, like me, wanting to say more. Finally, the *ding* came again, and the phone buzzed in my hand.

Have a good swim Ruth

Thank you

Talk to you tonight

I set the phone down on the bedside table and wandered to the bathroom. I examined my bedhead hairdo and wondered if I could fix it before Skyping tonight so it would look like it had leaving the salon. Not likely. Its natural inclination toward curly-wavy-chaos had been amplified by a night of sleep. I yanked it up into a ponytail and called it a day.

I found my swimsuit, pulled it on, grabbed a towel and my flip-flops, and tried to open and close the door into the hallway as quietly as possible. Five minutes later, I was in the water, doing sloppy but adequate doggy paddle laps from one end to the other.

Every time my mind wandered to Jack, I'd start counting backwards from twenty as a distraction. After about a dozen repetitions of this, I set myself to thinking about other things, anything. David. My mother. Kay. Bernie.

Bernie. Bernie who had moved to BC. Whose wife died a long time ago, so long ago that the woman at the cottage had never met her because she'd already been gone by the time she was born. Bernie, who Kay had been in love with.

Do you think about finding him? I had asked. *Every single day.* That's what she'd said. She thinks about him every single day. I let my feet touch the bottom of the pool and stood up, my shoulders and chest coming up out of the water. I pulled myself out of the pool and grabbed my towel, wiping my face as I walked toward the door.

If Kay was allowed to have a list with twenty-one-and-counting things on it, I was allowed to have a list with one thing: find Bernie. This was the Google era; how hard could it be?

※

Turned out it wasn't hard at all.

Bernie Kowalski, seventy-one, lending a hand at the local pancake breakfast, seen here with fellow Rotarians Jim Walsh and Dev Gill.

Bernie Kowalski attending city council to present his objections to expansion of the local ski hill.

Bernie Kowalski volunteering with the local hiking club to clean up a flood-damaged trail.

Bernie Kowalski playing his guitar at a local fundraiser for the high school's music program.

God, you had to love small-town newspapers. And love people who were involved in their community so much that they appeared in the paper's pages, frequently. Bernie had been in the newspaper at least once or twice a year over the last several years, and for various reasons. I scanned the photos and articles, looking for the golden ticket: an email address.

I googled "Kowalski" and "city council" to see if I could get more on his presentation at the council meeting. It didn't take long to find the PDF of the city council agenda and subsequent minutes, and there, in black and white, was what I was looking for: Bernie's email address, noted under contact information as a scheduled delegation to the council.

"Bingo," I whispered. I copied and pasted the address into the body of an email and sent it to myself. If I was going to send him a message, I needed to think about what I was going to say—and with Kay moving around in the room next door, my time had run out. I closed my laptop and grinned. I'd keep it a secret, for a surprise. She was going to be so excited.

※

We were on the road again by ten, a crappy continental breakfast at the hotel just enough to tide us over till a snack break along the road.

"Okay, my trusty navigator who insists on using maps instead of her phone—where should we head to tonight?"

"Well, David's original suggestion for today was arriving in Winnipeg; he suggested the Ramada a block off Highway 1," said Kay, deadpan.

I looked at her and snorted out a laugh. "We'd have to drive for … I don't even know, until tomorrow morning, to make it to Winnipeg," I said. "It's at least twenty-four hours from here."

"And I'm far too elderly and frail for *that*," Kay added, laughing. "Definitely."

She unfolded the map and smoothed it out over the portion of Ontario where we were. She ran her finger over the lines and shapes. "We can do Sault Ste. Marie in about four hours. Thunder Bay would be … I don't know, maybe twelve hours. What if we have a short day today, to Sault Ste. Marie, then get up early tomorrow and try for Thunder Bay?"

I thought about it a moment and nodded. Yes, that would work. Tomorrow would be rough but possible, and another big day after that would get us to Winnipeg, so we weren't too far behind David's original timeline.

The delays made me anxious. The country grew and stretched under us—the farther we drove, the more there was ahead, it seemed. The task of getting from one coast to the other had seemed straightforward. We even had a single highway that would do the job. But we'd been on the road a week and we weren't even halfway, and the long, empty prairies were still ahead. And on the other side of those prairies? BC, where David was waiting. And maybe Bernie too.

I glanced over at Kay. She had her list out again. From here it looked like about a third of it was checked off. "Read me the rest of the list, then," I said. I'd scanned the entire thing that first day in the diner, but I hadn't absorbed all of it enough to be certain of what remained.

"All right, we still have to watch a mountain sunrise or sunset, go dancing, have great sex," said Kay. She paused there and looked at me sideways.

"What? You or me?" I asked. "The sex, I mean."

"Hypothetically, it's open-ended. I had meant me, but hey, if you meet a cute fellow in a hotel lounge one night, who am I to say no."

"Yeah, but it says *great* sex. You're not going to get great sex from a stranger in a bar."

"You have a distinct lack of imagination, my friend," Kay grinned at me. "Speaking of which …."

She reached back to the floor behind our seats, pulled out the black shopping bag that she'd carried home from the sex store in Quebec City and started digging through it.

"Oh, Jesus," I said.

"Well, we never decided which one was mine and which one was yours," she said, her face innocent.

"I don't want one."

"You need one," she insisted.

"I really don't."

"Well, it's a gift, so … are you rejecting a gift from an old lady?"

"You're really playing up the old lady thing today, eh? You're not old by any measure."

"Can you tell my son that when we get to Vancouver?"

My laugh hitched into a gulping hiccup. Seeing David had been an abstract concept, but when Kay said it like that, it suddenly seemed real, and close. Maybe it was good that there was still so far to drive. Praise hallelujah for wide prairies and tall mountains.

Kay reached into the bag and pulled out two boxes, each about the size of a small umbrella folded up tight. She cleared her throat, then read the details of the labels like the announcer on *The Price is Right* describing a new luxury prize car.

"This, Ruthie, is the Lusty Nights XL. Eight inches of pleasure, seven vibration settings with both vaginal and clitoral stimulation, rechargeable and easy to clean. Also, it is a beautiful turquoise colour and looks like a dolphin. Sort of."

I was giggling, listening to her, and the dolphin pushed it over the edge. "A dolphin!"

She continued: "Behind Door 2, dear guest, we have Ride 'Em Cowgirl. Seven inches and ten vibration modes, also featuring dual clitoral and vaginal stimulation, for the discerning cowgirl. It is a beautiful tan colour and looks ... well, it looks like a penis. Not a dolphin."

"Oh my God, Kay," I laughed.

"Door 1 or Door 2, Ruthie, what's it going to be."

"I don't know!"

"Choose, or I'll choose for you," she said.

"Okay, the dolphin, the dolphin!"

"I knew you wanted that extra inch, you pervert," she grinned at me.

"No! It's just that the other one is very ... real looking. It's my first *thing* like this. Starting simple, Kay!"

"Vibrating dolphin it is, then."

She reached into the bag and pulled out what looked like a small bottle of shampoo. "This is sex toy cleaner. The girl recommended it. Apparently it'll help your 'product' last longer, and it's good for the pH of your lady zone."

"My lady zone?"

"That's what she called it. I think she meant vagina, but I can't keep up with the kids these days."

It made me happy, even though I was sort of the butt of the joke, to see her so amused.

"Wait, Ruthie, there's more," she said, reaching into the bag again.

She pulled out ... something. It was lacy, and small, and pink.

"It's, well, like a slip, sort of. A little dress, kind of. But stretchy."

It didn't look like there was enough fabric in her hand for a pair of panties, let alone a "little dress." I made a "hmph" sound in my throat.

"You can try it on later," she said.

"Fashion show?" I said, laughing.

"Oh, I don't need to see it, no. But I bet it'll look really sexy."

"On me?" I snorted. "Not likely."

"You're very hard on yourself, you know. For no reason. You're a smart, funny, good-looking woman—and you talk about yourself like you're a dorky fourteen-year-old with a face full of pimples and two left feet."

I stayed quiet for a moment, then frowned. "Well, I usually feel *exactly* like a dorky fourteen-year-old with two left feet. So I guess it makes sense that I talk about myself that way, right?"

"You should stop. What a waste of time and energy. In twenty years, you'll be looking at photos of yourself today and wondering why the hell you thought there was anything wrong. Trust me on this."

"Maybe," I said grudgingly.

"We're really nuts, you know. Women. We spend the first half of our lives trying to fix all the things that we think are wrong with us, then the second half wishing we'd realized there was nothing wrong to begin with. And by then our hips are starting to hurt, and we're getting wrinkles and going gray, and suddenly that thing we spent so long worrying about—our small boobs or our big nose—seems like nothing at all."

"I don't have a big nose," I said.

"Oh Ruthie, good Lord. I didn't mean *you*. I meant in general. You don't have small boobs either, not that there's anything wrong with small boobs. Mine are small, and I don't recall any man I ever got naked in front of complaining about them."

"Hordes of them, were there?" I said, laughing.

"There were enough," she said.

"Well, you did seem to know your way around the Dungeon in Quebec," I said.

She smiled and looked out the window. "Well, I had some very … interesting boyfriends. Before I met David's father, of course."

"What was he like?"

"Bill? He was very solid. Very certain and solid and calm. He always knew what to do next, how to fix a leaky tap in the middle of the night, what to say to David to get him to help with the chores with minimal grumbling. I loved him very much."

I kept my hands on the steering wheel, focusing on Kay but also on navigating my way around a slow-moving vehicle ahead of us, changing into the left lane and then back over into the right.

Kay continued talking in my silence. "We lived in Ontario for a couple of years when we were newly married. Bill travelled a lot for work," she said.

"Did you like it there?"

"Yes. It was a strange time, but a good one. It's a long story."

Long story, again. Code for I don't want to talk about this right now.

"So how did you end up in PEI from Ontario?" I asked, rerouting the conversation.

"Bill was from PEI, and one day his father had a stroke. His mother was alone, and the farm needed someone to work it. Bill arranged for a hired hand to help for a few days, and we closed up the apartment and cancelled our lease. We didn't have much stuff anyway; it all fit in the car. I didn't even get to say goodbye to anyone, really. Bill's mother passed a few years after that, and we kept the farm till Bill decided to retire, and then we sold off most of the fields to the farmer next to us and kept just the acreage around the house. It was a nice time, in its way, to just have our own little lot to worry about—the garden, the yard. Then everything happened with David and Melissa, and a couple years later, Bill passed away—heart attack—and … well, I got along fine, but

David didn't like it. I fractured my ankle last year, going down to the basement, and I made a joke to David about how I might have died down there if I couldn't get myself up the stairs—and that was it. From then on, it was just, 'Mom, it's time to move in with me,' and 'Mom, we're going to sell the farm.' Didn't matter what I said."

She was quiet for a moment and then sighed.

"I don't want to complain about having a son who loves me that much," she said. "But I didn't want to do this, you know?" She waved out at the passing scenery, and I looked over at her and half smiled, trying to show I understood. But did I, actually? Could I possibly know what it felt like to lose so many people? I'd lost Jack but not to death—to his own idiocy, or mine really, which wasn't the same as losing him. In fact, in a way, it was like being saved before it was too late. What if we'd carried on, indefinitely, while I pretended everything was great and wonderful? At least this way I was free, totally free, to do whatever I wanted.

"I didn't really want to do this either, Kay," I said. "It was a way to escape the island, and Jack."

"I know," she replied.

"But I'm really glad we're here, anyway."

"Of course you are; who wouldn't want a thrilling visit to exotic Sault Ste. Marie?"

I looked over at her and laughed. "I hope the hotel has a pool."

"We shall soon find out," she said, pointing ahead at a sign on the side of the road.

Sault Ste. Marie—forty kilometres. Thank God. I was ready to rest. And to write an email to the long-lost Bernie and hope it would land in the right inbox.

16

A FEW LONG DAYS of driving and we'd made it through Thunder Bay and into Winnipeg. The route was, in its way, beautiful: sparse and stark, with endless horizons of low evergreens, dotted with the autumn leaves of deciduous trees here and there. Small towns, some with no more than a gas station and truck stop, broke the sense of isolation at random intervals and gave us small goal posts to reach. But the days had been grinding—heavy truck traffic and long periods of silence. We were both feeling the bone-deep ache of sitting for too long day after day. When we pulled into Winnipeg at last, my body sagged with relief: we could stop soon.

At the hotel, I'd dropped my bags and gone straight for the shower. I was just stepping out of the bathroom, hair wrapped up in a towel, when Kay knocked at my door. She held her phone up and wiggled it. "I'm talking to David; he asked if we could do a video thingy, but my phone is almost dead. Can we use your laptop, Ruthie?"

"Oh," I said, looking down at my tank top and flannel pajama bottoms. "Sure, okay, yes." I pulled the laptop out of its bag and set it up on the desk; before our fight, Jules had found her older spare laptop and wiped it clean for me, reloaded useful programs and got it ready for me to use on the trip. Right now I wasn't sure if I was glad for her generosity after all.

"Okay, tell David we'll call by Skype in about five seconds."

Kay repeated this to him.

"And then hang up," I said.

"Oh, apparently I'm supposed to hang up now, hon. I'll see you in a minute," she said.

I clicked the screen open and hit the right buttons, then scooted out of the seat, shooing Kay into the spot. I didn't want David to see me like this, unprepared and looking drab and blah. Not that I spent a lot of time on my appearance on the best of days lately, but this was next-level casual. Also: no bra.

The ringing came to an abrupt end, and David's slightly pixelated face appeared on the screen. Kay waved. "Hi, hon!"

"Hi, Mom," he said. "You look great. Are you having fun? Is everything okay?"

"Everything is fantastic. We're having some great adventures. This might be the last time I see the whole country, so I may as well enjoy the view along the way."

It was meant to be funny, but I could tell—watching from the side—that the notion of Kay having a "last time" at something was distressing to David.

"Don't say stuff like that, Mom."

She shrugged, mollified. She hadn't intended to poke his soft spots, but she knew she had. "I'm sorry. You know what I mean, love."

"Yes."

I could tell David was leaning over his desk, staring closely at the screen on his side.

"You do look really great, Mom. Your hair looks awesome. Ruth is doing a great job, isn't she?"

"Ruthie? Yes, she's fantastic. She's a total pain in the butt and doesn't want to do anything dangerous or exciting or dramatic *ever*, but I'm working on her."

"No!" he said, laughing. "Sounds like she's just right as she is. Don't change her at all."

They both chuckled, then started talking at the same time, a result of the slight delay in the video connection, so neither knew the other was about to speak.

"How is work going—"

"Is Ruth right there—"

Their words overlapped, but I heard him ask for me. He always said Ruth, never Ruthie—which ought to have felt formal and distant but for some reason didn't at all, like it was a special nickname that only he used.

"Yes, she is," said Kay. "Hold on." I started to mouth *no, no, no, no,* but she'd already picked up the laptop and turned it toward me, plunking it in my lap where I sat cross-legged on the bed. She leaned forward in front of the camera and waved. "It is time for this old dame to go to bed. You kids have fun; don't stay up late, and no soda pop after ten." She chuckled to herself, enjoying her own joke, and blew a kiss into the camera. "Good night, hon."

She stood so that David could no longer see her, and then looked at me. She grinned and pointed at the screen, followed by an exaggerated swoony-kissy type of face, and my eyes went wide. I wanted to tell her to get stuffed, but it seemed inadvisable with her son—and technically my employer—on the screen right in front of me. "Okay then, thanks, Kay. Good night," I said, my voice tight.

She left the room, pulling the door shut behind her. I looked back at the screen. I could see a small version of myself in the upper right corner, the screen-in-screen showing me what I looked like on David's end. From the small version, it looked like it was all boobs and towel head. Fantastic.

"Hi," he said.

"Hi," I replied.

"So, everything is going well?"

"Yes, so far so good. Your mom is a lot of fun."

"Yes, she can be. Sometimes too much," he said, smiling a little.

"She'd say, 'But is there such a thing as too much fun?'" I replied.

"Yes, she would. You know her well."

I didn't answer but smiled back. Conversation with good-looking men was not my forté to begin with; add in the stilted nature of video calls and the fact that I was in my ratty pajamas, and I was doubly struggling.

"Did I interrupt your shower or …?" he asked, pointing toward the screen, obviously indicating my towel.

"No, no, I was already out. Just … lazy. I haven't brushed my hair yet is all." I pointed upwards, like he could miss the huge white dome on top of it.

"Okay," he said.

"So, what are you doing? Tonight, I mean?" Ugh. What? Why was I asking that?

"Tonight?"

"It's Friday. At least, I think it is. I'm losing track. No hot date?" *Oh my God, stop, Ruthie. Stop talking right now.*

His face froze for a moment, and I couldn't decide if he was mad or felt uncomfortable, or if the connection between our screens was just lagging. But he chuckled, finally, and said, "No. No hot date for me. Except with a stack of permit application paperwork."

"Permit applications?"

"A necessary evil of the job. I design things. Sort of. Well, it's complicated. But I make things that need to be approved, by governments and all sorts of agencies and organizations. Sometimes it feels like I need a nod of approval from everyone on the planet before we can go ahead. But that's just the nature of it. I like the engineering. The paperwork not so much. But they go together, right?"

I nodded. I really had no idea, but it sounded right.

"I think when I was in university, I imagined I was going to spend my time building wells in places that needed water, and basically being a hero. The reality is not so humanitarian, but it pays the bills—and employs a lot of people so they can pay their bills too."

"That's important. People need work to support their families."

"Yes."

There was a long silence then, and I wasn't sure what to do or say—but it didn't feel awkward. I enjoyed looking at him as he fiddled with a paper clip in his fingers and stared back at me.

"So …," he started.

"So …," I replied.

"No hot date there?" he asked.

I laughed. "Not part of my job description—this is a 24-7 gig."

"Wow, your boss must be a jerk."

"She's okay."

He laughed. "I meant me, but yeah. I guess she's the boss too, isn't she?"

"You have no idea."

"Hey, I grew up with her. Trust me, I have an idea," he said, laughing.

"Fair point."

"I know she doesn't want to come, and I feel like a jerk for insisting but … it's time. Better to do it before there's a bigger issue than afterwards," he said.

I nodded but didn't say anything. It seemed to me that Kay had many years ahead before anyone needed to worry about "a bigger issue." At thirty years my senior, she was twice as capable as me in pretty much every way—mentally, emotionally and even physically, for that matter.

"You don't agree?"

"It's not my job, or my place, to agree or disagree."

"I'm curious what your opinion is though, Ruth." His voice rumbled slow and deep when he said it, my name coming out like an entreaty, not a demand.

I paused for a moment, and I thought about what Kay had said on the back porch that night at her house, and about everything I'd seen since then. "I think there's more life in Kay than most people, of any age. I think she's got a lot of life still, and perhaps moving in with you makes her feel like what's left is short and not her own."

He made a noise, like a "hmm" in his throat.

"Are you mad?" I asked.

"No. And even if I was, that's okay. You're allowed to have your opinion, whether it differs from mine or not."

"I understand why you want her to come."

"Do you?"

"Your mom told me about … what happened, and …."

"Ah." His face changed, in the second it took for the "ah" to pass his lips, and suddenly his expression was somewhere between stern and blank.

"David, I—"

"I'd best get going here, Ruth. So thank you, again. Things are a little behind schedule, but everyone's safe, and that's what counts. We will see you here in Vancouver in a few more days, hopefully. Have a good night."

"David—"

The screen went black.

17

Subject: An Old Friend?
From: Ruth MacInnes <rmacinnes@sparkmail.com>
To: Bernie Kowalski <bernardgkowalski@telemail.com>
Dear Mr. Kowalski:
I sincerely hope I have the right email. I found it online by searching your name and your last-known town of residence. If this finds you in error, please disregard. I believe we have a friend in common: Kay March. I am currently travelling across Canada with her. As we have travelled through some "old stomping grounds," your name has come up. Since we are going to be travelling through your area, I was wondering if you would be interested in seeing an old friend again? Perhaps you can let me know if you are the right Bernie Kowalski?
Thank you,
Ruthie MacInnes

I hit *Send*, watched the email go from Outbox to Sent and grinned. I felt like a matchmaker, twirling destiny from my fingertips—who knew where this might go? "Or you've watched too many romantic comedies," I said to myself under my breath as I slid the laptop into its case and put it inside my luggage bag. I did a final check of the hotel room, brushed my hair, found my keys and sunglasses, and was just about to pull open the door when the email inbox on my phone buzzed. Instructions from David? More likely photos of my nieces and nephews from my sister. I set the bag down and pulled the phone out of my pocket.

"Re: An Old Friend." Oh my God. Already? I'd just sent it. It must have bounced back—bad email. I clicked on it.

> Dear Ms. MacInnes,
> Yes, you have the right email and the right person. I would be ecstatic to see Kay again, any time. I am still in the Rossland area, and yes, if you are travelling across the country, you would pass through here on the old highway, if you elected to leave the Trans-Canada. Please let me know at your earliest convenience when you might be arriving. BK

I didn't have time to respond right away but promised myself I would as soon as we made a pit stop. I'd found him. I'd *actually* found him.

✳

The next two days were a blur of driving, making pit stops to use the bathroom, and eating food from gas stations. The landscape had changed so dramatically, it was hard to believe we were still in the same country: there seemed to be more sky than land, the blue of it stretching wide in every direction over the gold-green fields. Occasional small, curving hills seemed like mountains compared to the flatness around us, and the farther west we travelled, the smaller and closer to the ground the trees and shrubs seemed to be. It was beautiful, though, wide open in a way that I'd never experienced growing up in Quebec or living in PEI all these years. I could almost imagine living in a place like this.

Kay had begun to talk about our Drumheller stop, informing me that we were going to spend two days in the small Alberta town so we could devote an entire day to the museum. I wasn't sure it would require an entire day, but she'd also registered us for a lengthy educational hike in the surrounding badlands. It struck me as the sort of thing that Kay would adore and that I would grumble my way through—and then later realize I'd actually had a great time. Why did I do that? Complain up front, then discover I'd enjoyed myself. Like I was always assuming that things would go south, and everything would be awful. Had I always been that way?

I'd spent most of Manitoba letting my mind wander over questions like this—about myself, and about Jack, my sister, my parents, David, Kay. I spent several hours thinking about Jules, and at the next gas station, I pulled my phone out to send her a text, but then I deleted it. She hadn't messaged me since I'd left, and it had been several weeks since we'd fought in the pub. Maybe she was still mad. Maybe I should let her decide when and if she wanted to talk to me again. Maybe I'd just wait till I got back home—if I went back there at all.

It was hard to imagine going "back home." PEI wasn't really my home so much as the place I had landed for an extended period. Without Jack-ass—and on top of that, without Jules—and with no job waiting for me, there wasn't a reason to return. But going back to Shawville and my family seemed worse, in a way—not that I didn't love the place, but if I went back there, I wasn't sure I'd ever leave again, sinking into the comfort of my old bed, my old home, my old life. I was too old for that now, as tempting as it was. So, where?

I had no idea—which was equal parts terrifying and exciting. This job would give me enough money to take time to find a job somewhere and then get there, too. This job was going to save my butt, frankly. How much longer could I have hung out, miserable and hungover, on the couch in Jules's apartment?

My car was still there, of course, but that could be sorted out if necessary. It was hardly a dream vehicle, and the clutch was likely to go in the next year anyway. What if I landed somewhere that had public transit and I didn't need a car? A big city, somewhere I could just walk wherever I needed to go? Or a really small town, where everything was in close quarters? What if I stayed in Vancouver and got a bike? It only snowed there like, what, every ten years?

It was somewhere after Moose Jaw but before Swift Current when I heard the first funny click—not that I realized it was a funny click at the time. It was just a background noise, but my brain registered it in between my wandering thoughts, and later, another hundred kilometres up the road, when the single click turned into a constant click-click-click-click and then almost immediately into a roaring whomp-whomp-whomp-whomp. I pulled over. Kay and I looked at each other.

"That's not good," said Kay.

I frowned, pulled on the hood release and got out of the car slowly, like the van was a mysterious package in a train station and it *might* be a bomb about to go off. There were soft tendrils of grey steam-smoke coming up around the edge of the hood. I got my fingers under it, flipped the latch to the side and pulled up, releasing a mushroom cloud of smoke in the process.

"Oh shit."

Kay had hopped out by then, and when the smoke had mostly cleared, we leaned over the engine in unison, searching for clues. "Do you have any idea what we might be looking for?" I asked, hoping that Kay's seemingly endless bag of lived wisdom would include "engine troubles," as it had included so many other things.

"Not a clue," she replied.

"Me neither." Still, we looked, brows furrowed, poking and pointing: Was that oil? Was it a leak? Where did the coolant go in? Maybe it was low? Transmission? I threw out random words as though somehow I would be able to download the user manual on the minivan from some cosmic source. But after another three minutes of staring into the engine's mysterious components, I had to conclude I had literally no idea what the problem might be.

"Okay, we need to figure out exactly where we are and then find a mechanic." I pulled out my phone and got busy looking up the map to find us with the GPS, then googled for information about the next town up the road.

It took less time to find a mechanic shop than it had taken me to stare blankly at the engine. I called the number and explained to the guy on the other end what was going on, and he promised to be there with a tow truck "soon."

"What does 'soon' mean in the middle of nowhere," I said to Kay after I hung up.

"Your guess is as good as mine."

"I think we're going to be here a while," I replied.

"Yep."

I looked west along the highway, then back behind us toward the east. Nothing. Just pavement, grassy ditch, wire fencing with wood posts marking off the distance every fifteen metres or so, and fields of … something. Wheat? Canola? Who knew? "It is beautiful, isn't it?"

"It really is," Kay agreed.

I climbed back into the car, and Kay followed suit. The second she was settled, she pulled her list out of her pocket and grabbed a pen from the dashboard. "I'm making an addition."

"What? We don't even have half of them done as it is! No additions," I said.

"Trust me."

I leaned over and watched as she spelled out a new item at the bottom: #22—teach Ruthie how to play crib.

I smiled. "All right, that's a fair addition. I'll allow it."

Kay laughed. "You'll allow it, eh? Well, by all means, if her highness approves."

"All right, where's your board?" I asked.

Kay twisted in her seat, reached behind me and pulled out a small bundle tied around its middle with a string. "In here," she said, pulling on the small bow and unwinding the fabric, which appeared to be a small and very well-worn child's quilt. The board was small, the length and width of a loaf of bread, but only two inches in depth. She handed it to me, then refolded the quilt and set it aside.

As I had the first time I'd seen it, I let my fingers run over the wood. The track of holes had three "lanes" in a long oval, like a racetrack, around the middle of the board. The outer edges of the board had been carved in the shapes of leaves and pine cones, as though the track was set down in a patch of forest floor that had been cleared away. I ran my fingers over the board, feeling the intricate details of each shape and curve. "It's so beautiful."

"A friend made it for me a very long time ago." She took the board back from me then and flipped it over, revealing a small inset drawer that popped out, revealing the playing pieces and a deck of cards.

"BWK," I said, pointing at the initials I had noticed the first time.

Kay didn't say anything, just continued by flipping the board back over and placing our pieces in the starting slots, balancing the board on the edges of our two seats so it lay between us like a piece of lumber over a small creek. As she started shuffling, I realized that the initials must be Bernie's. Bernie Kowalski. Middle name something that began with W: Walter. Wayne. William.

"Did Bernie make this for you?"

Kay smiled. "Yes, he did."

"He's very talented."

"Yes, he was. He was a carpenter; he made all sorts of things—chairs and bookshelves, anything that could be made out of wood."

"But this is not carpentry; this is something an artist would make," I said.

"Well, I think a great many carpenters are artists, but yes, it's wood carving, and he was very skilled and very talented." She was silent for a moment. "I watched him make it. It took days and days, of course, and I didn't see it all, but I watched him do a good portion of it. We were at the cottage in winter for a few days. Back then there was no TV or telephones; they'd only just gotten electricity to the cottage a year or two before. He'd built the cabin frame with wiring, knowing that eventually the transmission lines would come that far. So for the first couple years, there were light fixtures in the ceiling and switches and a place for a fridge—but no power. All the heat was from the woodstove, and there were only candles for light."

Kay kept shuffling the cards, and I didn't say a word, fearful that I'd interrupt her, and she'd stop. I wanted to hear more.

"I didn't know it was for me till he'd finished it and gave it to me."

"He sounds really great," I said.

"He was," she replied. "I loved David's father very much. But Bernie was the love of my life." She kept her eyes on the cards, shuffling them back and forth in her hands, but I could hear in her voice that she was trying to keep tears at bay. She looked up then and gave me a half smile. "If you tell David that, I will fire you," she said, and laughed.

"I won't."

"All right, so cut for high card, and the winner deals first," she said, holding out the deck for me.

I reached out and lifted off the top half of the deck, flipping it over to reveal the queen of hearts.

"That's a good one," Kay said. She cut lower down and flipped over a five of spades. "You deal first."

"Okay, but you're going to have to tell me what to do. I mean, everything. I haven't played in years and years."

She nodded and told me to deal out six cards each. As I did, I saw her fingers touch the edge of the board, the tiniest gentle touch. The conversation had moved on, but she was still thinking about Bernie. And Bernie, thanks to my Google sleuthing, was probably thinking about her right now too.

18

"IT'S THE RADIATOR and I can fix it, but I don't have that part here. I have to order it in. Could be ... three days. It's Friday today, so there's the weekend. It's hard to say. Monday maybe, but not likely."

The mechanic just kept talking as Kay and I looked at each other, eyes getting wider and wider. We were in a town a few miles off the highway, the sort of place where you might film a movie about a small town, with prop guys throwing tumbleweeds into the scene from off-camera: a single main street, a small grid of older houses with tidy yards, three churches, a gas station and a handful of businesses. I knew there was also, somewhere, a school and a library because I'd seen the signs for them pointing off the main street as we'd come into town.

"You could have it towed ahead to Moose Jaw. But that'd cost a few hundred. Or more, on a Friday afternoon. There's a motel, end of the main drag, and I can call ahead for you; my sister owns it. It's not fancy, but it's all right."

He stared at us. I looked at Kay and sighed. "David is going to be so pissed."

"Bugger it. We can't control the bloody radiator," said Kay, rolling her eyes. She turned back to the mechanic: "Is there a bar or anything like that in town?"

"No, there's a few places to eat here, but if you want a bar, there's one about five miles over, next town. It's pretty good, sometimes live music on a weekend."

"All right then, we'll stay till the part arrives. I don't suppose there's taxis around, if we wanted to go out one night to this place?"

"No, but if you let my sister know you want to go, I'm sure she'd take you over."

Kay looked at me and nodded. "Perfect—#13 go dancing, and #6 get drunk."

"Kay …."

The mechanic—Randy—looked back and forth between us.

"If we're stuck, we're stuck, right?"

It was hard to argue the logic. I looked at Randy and shrugged. "Okay, we'll stay till the part arrives. We'll just get the bags we need out of the van."

"Sure, get what you want, and I'll drive you up to the motel," he answered.

I nodded a thank you and turned to Kay. "You're telling David."

❋

By nightfall we were settled in adjacent rooms at the almost-empty Sleepy Inn Motel. We had called David to explain the situation, walked up to the closest restaurant for dinner, and then spent an hour sitting cross-legged on my bed as Kay beat me at ten rounds of cribbage in a row.

"This game is not really very fun," I said, sighing and rolling myself off the bed.

"It's great fun; you're just losing," she said.

"Yeah, well, that too. I'm going to go get a soda from the machine; do you want one?"

"No thanks, love."

I wandered outside. It was the sort of motor hotel where you pull your car right up to the door. It had a long row of matching doors with matching door mats, and matching patio chairs sat next to each one. There was a Coke machine outside the front office. It was chilly but clear, an autumn night on the prairie. In a few hours, the stars would be crystal clear, I imagined—right now, the last tinge of sunset was still on the horizon, the sky a velvet blue not yet descended into the navy ink it would become.

I put my change in the machine and got a single can of Coke, then wandered back to my room. My phone buzzed in my pocket just as I got to the door.

A text from David: *Sorry about the van. I'm sure this delay was not expected, and I hope it will not impact your plans afterwards.*

We were back to formal texts, complete with proper punctuation.

It's no problem, I wrote back. *I don't have a set date I need to be finished and I'm not yet sure of my plans after.*

I stuck my head in the door and told Kay I was going to sit outside and look at the sky for a bit, and she came outside with the crib board under her arm.

"I figured we were done for the night," she said. "I tidied everything up. Rematch tomorrow."

"Sure. You can kick my ass another dozen times by noon."

"Nope. I saw a sign on the window at the restaurant. The Episcopal church is having a book sale tomorrow morning, so I will be out shopping for novels," she answered.

"Mind if I sleep in and skip the book sale?"

"Of course. You need your rest if we're going out tomorrow night."

"Seriously? Dancing?" I asked, wrinkling up my nose—realizing even as I did it how much of a bore I sounded like.

"Dancing. And shots." She beamed.

"Um. We'll see."

"It's happening, Ruthie. The list! The list is king."

I smiled at her. "Okay, tomorrow night. Dancing. And maybe *one* shot." My phone buzzed in my hand, and I lifted it to see. David had replied. I smiled.

"I'll leave you to your conversation," she said. "He's a pain in the butt, my son, but he's a good egg."

"Oh, I'm not … it's not … we're just … it's about, you know, the trip."

How had she known? But then, in all the time we'd been travelling, I'd had very few messages or calls from anyone *other* than David. So yeah, *of course* it was David.

"Good night," she said, throwing a hand over her shoulder as she walked to her door. "Be good."

I dropped into the patio chair next to my door and set the Coke at my feet, unopened. I was too chilly now for a cold drink. I'd save it for later. I turned my attention back to the phone.

Oh, I assumed you'd be heading straight home?

I paused a moment, figuring out the best way to word a reply. *No. I'm not sure yet. I might but it may be a good time to relocate somewhere.*

Wouldn't you miss anyone there?

No. I broke up with my boyfriend a few months ago. My family is all in Quebec. And I was living with my best friend, but she doesn't really have room for me. So I don't really have anyone I need to get back to.

Oh. I didn't realize. I just figured someone would be waiting on you to return.

No.

There was silence for a minute after that. Was that the end of the conversation? I'd sounded like an idiot, obviously. I shouldn't have said all that stuff. I looked up at the sky and saw the first few stars twinkling overhead. On the other side of the parking lot, a pair of teenagers passed by, walking along the edge of the highway, their hands held and swinging between them, their low voices and laughter carrying across the still night.

I couldn't remember the last time I'd held hands with someone or gone for a walk together. Teenagers in small-town Saskatchewan had a better love life than me. I looked back down at the screen. He hadn't replied yet. I was just about to get up and go back inside when it buzzed again.

Have you thought about staying out here?

I stared at the screen. It was idle curiosity on his part, I knew, but still I wanted to read it as, "I'd *like* it if you stayed out here."

Foolish of me, but I couldn't help wishing that was what he meant by it.

Yes, I replied.

I think you'd really like it. It rains a lot, but it's beautiful.

It looks it. I'm sure I'll stay for a while, get a hotel, sightsee. I guess it all depends on what I decide to do next.

Hotels here are very expensive.

Oh, good to know. Maybe not, then.

There's lots of room here at my place.

I didn't respond right away, just stared at his words on the screen. I didn't want to jump to conclusions, or into more bad decisions. And right now I could do both, easily.

Up to you, I mean.

Okay. Thank you. Bedtime here I think. Good night.

I shut the phone off and went inside to get ready for bed.

✳

Kay had returned from the Good Shepherd Episcopal Annual Book and Bake Sale with six Nora Roberts romance novels, a *Taste of Home Christmas* cookbook and a handful of *Archie* comics, plus a plate of poppyseed strudel and a half-dozen bran muffins. She convinced me to take one of the romance novels, though I insisted I didn't read them, and then she cut up the strudel and set a piece for each of us on paper plates.

Randy had phoned already to let us know the part was ordered, and a friend of a friend of a friend was going to pick it up in Moose Jaw and bring it here tomorrow, saving probably two days in delivery, so he could start working on it late Sunday or first thing Monday morning. We'd likely be good to go by Tuesday.

"Well, on the upside, we could use the break from the road, and now you can't argue with me about going out tonight," Kay chuckled. "We have days to recover."

"I guess so," I said.

I felt genuine anxiety about the entire idea. I didn't have anything to wear (though when I noted this to Kay, she looked around and said, "We're in the middle of Saskatchewan; it's not Fashion Week in Paris, kiddo," to which I had to acknowledge that yes, probably, my jeans and a sweater would do just fine).

But a bar always had men in it. And sometimes they wanted to talk to you. Or dance with you, even. ("You can just say, 'No, thank you,'" Kay reminded me.)

I'd been putting back a ton of wine—or whatever else was available—for months at home, but I hadn't had so much as a sip in weeks now. What if I had a couple shots and barfed? ("Just have one, then, a symbolic wild night," said Kay, getting frustrated.) After some more general grumbling on my part, Kay gathered up the books and the muffins and the remaining strudel and said she was heading back to her own room to read.

"I talked to Diane, and she says she can give us a ride over any time after six, and we can call her for a ride back before midnight," said Kay. Diane was the owner of the motel, sister to Randy the mechanic. "So, be ready at six."

I didn't respond.

"Think of it this way: we'll never get #20 accomplished if we don't mix and mingle a little," Kay said.

"What's #20 again?"

Kay moved her body in a cross between a tango and an Elvis hip thrust.

"Ugh," I said.

"The trip will feel incomplete if we don't do everything."

"Yeah, but do you really want some one-night stand in a country bar in the middle of Saskatchewan just to say you've crossed it off your list?"

Kay pursed her lips, and her arms gripped her stack of books tighter, the muffins balanced on top. "Well, not really, Ruthie, but

I'm sure you know that without asking. I just want to have a good time, while there's time to still have it."

The way she frowned and blinked made me think she was about to cry. I didn't want to be responsible for making her cry. It wasn't *my* fault. It was hers, for this whole ridiculous idea of having a list in the first place.

Well, maybe there's time yet ahead of us, I thought, thinking of Bernie.

"Once the car is fixed, we're only a few days from David's."

"Well, it's not like your life ends the second we arrive there, Kay. You might meet lots of new people, do new things."

"Yeah," she replied. "I know. I guess it's the point of the thing. Just … be ready at six."

She turned and left before I could say anything else, and as soon as the door swung closed, I wanted to run out and apologize. Then I felt defensive: apologize for what, I thought to myself, being a realist?

I sat down on the bed, opened the laptop and logged in. There was an email from Bernie. And another one from David. And, to my surprise, a third one from Jack.

19

AT 5:45 P.M. I pulled on my cleanest jeans, a T-shirt and a hoodie with the words Prince Edward Island across the front, the style of the font like an old-fashioned varsity shirt. I put on my shoes and then backtracked to the bathroom and leaned over the sink to look at myself. "Okay, don't be an asshole. Pretend you want to do this."

I pulled out eyeliner and lipstick, and when those were applied, I dug deeper into the bag and found the mascara, adding a layer to each set of eyelashes. I reached up and pulled my ponytail out, letting my hair come down.

What would Jack think of how I looked? What would David think? Did it matter what either of them thought? What did I think?

I thought I looked all right. I thought I looked healthy. Sane. I hadn't been drunk in weeks. My skin looked better than it had in ages, that ruddy thing on my cheeks from the booze all gone. My hair was washed. My clothes weren't fancy, but they were tidy.

I looked cute, actually. Not "twenty years old and fresh as a summer's day" cute, but "this is me, and I'm all right" cute. I smiled at myself in the mirror and it felt … normal. How many times had I laughed with Kay in the last few weeks? How many times had I laughed in the six months prior to that combined?

I felt lighter, like I'd lost the heavy backpack I'd been carrying around. I wanted to tell myself it was all me, some inner well of strength and new-found wisdom, because isn't that how growth is supposed to happen? But honestly, it was, at least a little bit, the emails that had arrived earlier.

Jack's had been short and sweet. He hoped I was well. He'd heard through the grapevine about the job and the trip across the country, and he hoped I was having fun and seeing new things. He added, like an afterthought, that he just wanted to let me know that he and Carly (Flower Shop Girl had a name, I guess) had decided to get married, and he knew that would be hard to hear, but he wanted me to know before I returned home.

He didn't apologize for what he had done—though if I was being honest, he had apologized, sort of, in the past. I had hit reply and sent:

> Jack,
> The job is great, and the trip has been a good chance to see some new places. We are in Saskatchewan currently. To be honest, I'm not sure if I'll be coming back to PEI after I'm done here, but it's all up in the air right now. Thank you for letting me know your exciting news. Congratulations. I mean that, sincerely. I hope you will be very happy.
> Good luck with everything,
> Ruth

And by the time I'd written the words "I mean that," I was surprised to discover that I really *did* mean it. I switched over to my Facebook account and—as I had so many times over the last few months—navigated to Jack's profile and let my finger hover over "unfriend." But this time, at last, I clicked it, and suddenly his profile was closed to me. It felt strange, but not sad or frightening or awful, as I'd imagined it would.

Was it being far away that made it easier? Was it being sober? Was it time—which heals all, after all, right? Was it David, or more accurately, the *idea* of David? Just interacting with him these last weeks had been a reminder that Jack was not, in fact, the last man on the planet. If I was enjoying David's company, how much of that was because I genuinely liked David—and how much was the simple pleasure of a bit of mystery and flirtation and *newness*?

David's email had been a surprise too, in its own way. Most of our communication was done by text, phone call or sometimes Skype. So to see his name in my inbox had surprised me. It was a simple note, and two photos.

> Ruth,
>
> I just wanted to reiterate the invitation to stay here with us after you both arrive. I know people often think such invitations are just politeness, but I truly mean it. I'm attaching two photos—one of the spare room you could stay in, and one of the backyard. It's a bit grey and drab out there today, but it is quite lovely; the patio has a cover over it, and it's a nice place to sit and have a coffee and think. Perhaps you would even like to go ahead over to Vancouver Island, so you could say you'd gone coast to coast, and then return to my house for a time. I'm very close to the SkyTrain line, so it's easy to get around, and you could spend some time sightseeing. Please don't worry about food or anything like that; I would be very happy to have you as my guest.
>
> So that's all I wanted to say—and thank you for everything and for being with my mom. I can tell she's really enjoying herself. It makes me wish I was on the trip with you guys and not here in my office staring out at the rain.
>
> I hope I will talk to you soon.
>
> David
>
> PS I always enjoy our conversations very much.

It was the last line that really did it, of course. "I always enjoy our conversations very much." For someone as serious and formal as David, this felt like a massive statement. Was I over-reading it, though?

I looked at myself in the mirror again and imagined pulling in at David's house for the first time, getting out of the car and smiling at him. I smiled at myself in the mirror as I imagined it. What would he think of me in real life? What would I think of him? It seemed so far away but terrifyingly close. Not enough time to, say, have a complete makeover, I thought, plucking at the lint on my old hoodie.

"Good enough," I said out loud. Whether I meant good enough for David or good enough for our night out to the bar, I didn't really know. But I nodded at myself and headed to the door to meet Kay.

✳

Three hours later, I had enjoyed four shots of tequila and two beers, and I had been dancing for at least an hour straight. I was being careful, chugging glasses of ice water in between the rounds of shots. I'd long since removed the hoodie, had practically sweat through my T-shirt, and my face was bright red, but I didn't care.

"Kay, I'm sorry, you were right," I said, leaning across the table to yell at her over the music. She grinned up at me, her own face flushed and pink from the alcohol and the dancing.

A man who introduced himself as "Randy the Mechanic's brother-in-law Ted" had asked Kay to dance within a few minutes of arriving, and Kay had surprised me—and probably most of the bar, who had apparently heard who we were and why we were in town —by matching him step for step around the dance floor. She could two-step, waltz, line dance and just about anything else, apparently.

After that, it seemed that every man in the place had come to ask for a dance, keeping Kay on her feet until she begged off for a break, flopping down next to me in the booth.

The bar was nothing fancy—a replica of a hundred similar bars across the country, with old Miller Light neon signs on the walls, a pool table, dartboards, and an honest-to-goodness jukebox full of old Blue Rodeo and Bruce Springsteen and Hank Williams and lots of modern country singers I didn't recognize. But it was clean and well-maintained, and clearly well loved by its patrons, who all seemed to know one another, and who were determined to get to know us too. When the Tragically Hip's "Courage" came on, it seemed as though the entire bar moved en masse to the dance floor, shouting out the words in a group singalong. It was loud and chaotic and ridiculous—and the best fun I'd had in years.

"You were right," I said again. "This is awesome."

She laughed at me.

"Awesome," I said again, louder, like a cheer. I knew I was being goofy, and I didn't care. Someone tapped me on the shoulder, and when I turned I recognized him as "Randy the Mechanic's brother-in-law's best friend Adam." He put his hand out toward me and raised an eyebrow. I smiled back and let him pull me onto the dance floor. We were a few seconds into dancing when the song ended and, on cue, a slower song began. He twirled me in close, and I easily let myself be pulled up tight to his warm chest, feeling myself tucked in against him as we started to sway.

I wish I could say it was "Randy the Mechanic's brother-in-law's best friend Adam" I was thinking of when I closed my eyes, but it wasn't, of course.

It was David. David and *I always enjoy our conversations very much*. David with his photos of his green and rainy backyard and the spare room with the double bed and the white duvet and big, fluffy pillows. David with his invitations and his gentle, polite ways. Even his texting made me grin, the way he always used a comma where needed, and ended every sentence with a period. Was so serious, then cracked jokes in between.

Tipsy and giddy, I rested my head on Adam's shoulder and let my imagination carry me off. How tall was he? As tall as Adam? What did he smell like? Adam smelled okay—sweaty in a clean way, like he'd showered before coming here. David smelled better, I imagined.

When the song ended, I could tell Adam wanted to continue, but I insisted I needed to sit down and drink more water, so he escorted me back to the table and nodded at Kay before heading over to the pool table again.

I let myself fall into the booth next to her so we could both face outwards to the rest of the bar, people watching. It was easier to talk to each other this way, too, rather than yelling across the table.

"Where did you learn how to do all those dances?" I asked Kay.

"Well, I think it was a little more common in my generation to know how to do that. But I used to go dancing with my husband a fair bit, when we were younger. And Bernie and I danced often. Actually he taught me, really, most of it. I had some basics, but he was so good and enjoyed it so much. Sometimes we'd just put the radio on and dance to whatever came on." Bernie's name cropped up often now, as though once the seal had been removed the first time, she suddenly felt safe to talk about him.

"He sounds awesome," I said. *Awesome* was apparently my go-to word when drunk on tequila.

She grinned. "He really was."

For a split second it occurred to me that maybe I should let her know that I'd been in touch with Bernie, but I had it in my head that it was going to be a surprise, and truth be told I was no longer sure she would be so pleased about it. It was easier to just carry on with the plan, not think about it, and see what happened.

And yes, there was in fact a plan: the third email this afternoon had been from Bernie, a reply to my reply to his reply to my reply in a long string of emails that had been going back and forth over the last few days.

He had outlined in his last email that we could reroute from Highway 1, take the more southerly Crowsnest Highway on Route 3, and stop in Rossland for a visit—if we were so inclined. Pragmatically, he acknowledged that it was a tougher route to drive, but he added that it was more scenic, too, as though it was only fair to let us know both the pros and cons of coming that way. I had answered that yes, we'd both love it.

Both. I hadn't yet told him that Kay didn't know I had been in touch. In fact, I had made up a little white lie—that she didn't use email herself, and so she had asked me to do so on her behalf—and that yes, we'd be ecstatic to come for a visit and enjoy the scenic route along the way. So now I had to figure out how to divert from sticking to Highway 1 the whole way through, as we'd planned, and whether or not to tell her what I'd done—and when.

Think about it later, I thought to myself, a sudden clenching in my tummy evidence of my anxiety over what I'd done, or a sign I'd had too much tequila. Most likely both.

Kay must have noticed the sudden odd expression on my face and assumed I'd hit the booze-and-dancing wall. She leaned over to suggest it was time to head back. Diane, the motel owner and our impromptu taxi driver, had stayed at the bar all evening herself, and she was still chatting with friends on the other side of the room. She'd kept to soda all night, so I wasn't worried about her driving, and as Kay made her way over to ask her about leaving, I was relieved to be able to just let other people take care of me from here. Kay could get us organized, Diane would drive, and surely I could manage to get myself into bed. My head was spinning, and my body felt like it was buzzing.

Because it *was* buzzing. My phone was going off in my pocket: text notifications from David.

I hope you guys are having a good time. Not sure how often you check your email, but I sent you a message earlier.

I stared at the screen, my head swimming a little, and my heart beating fast.

We're AWESOME. We went out dancing.

With my mom? Is she okay?

It was her idea. She's a better dancer than me.

Oh.

Don't worry, we're heading back to the hotel now.

I'm not worried.

This was the point where, sober, I'd have not said anything and just wrapped the conversation up. But I had enough Miller and tequila in me to say things I wouldn't have otherwise.

Really? You sure?

Well, nervous I guess. I worry a little, yes.

You worry a LOT. Your mom is amazing you know.

I know, she really is.

I can see where you get it from.

Silence. I stared at the screen, but there was no reply. Too much? Then, suddenly: *Get what from?*

Your awesomeness.

Me?

Yes, silly, you.

A pause.

Have you been drinking?

I have, yes. A little. Your mom made me.

Are you okay to get back to the motel?

Yes, Diane will drive us. Adam and Ted will help us to the car if we need them to. LOL

Why did I say that? Like some weird high-school tactic to tell your crush you're hanging out with another boy?

Who are they?

Diane owns the motel, and Adam and Ted are your mother's dance partners. Oh, well, mine too I guess. Oh, time to go.

Kay had returned to the table with Diane. "All right you party girls, off we go then?"

I smiled up at Diane. "Yes please. Thank you!" When I stood up, my head started spinning double time, and I giggled and hiccupped at the same time. Like the town and the bar, I had become the drunk-girl movie version of myself.

Kay rolled her eyes at me. "You okay there, lightweight?"

"Lightweight? I had a *lot* of tequila, you know."

"I guess so. Okay, out we go."

On the way to the door, the other people in the bar waved good night, as though we were long-lost friends who'd popped in for a welcome visit. It made me miss the comfort of home, of knowing everyone at the coffee shop and the library and the grocery store— till I remembered Jack's email, and my stomach flip-flopped.

"So much for being over the Jack-ass," I said to myself, words slurring. Earlier tonight I'd felt so peaceful about Jack, and now here it all was rushing back at me. I felt my phone buzz again in my pocket a few times. David, probably, trying to check in with me. I'd respond when I got back to the motel, I decided, and I followed Kay and Diane out into the cool autumn night.

When I looked up, the sky was clear as could be, and the stars were a million pinpricks of light. I looked for the Big Dipper and Orion, and midway through trying to decide if I'd spotted Cassiopeia, I started to tilt backwards and nearly fell on my ass. Righting myself, I hurried to catch up to Kay and Diane, and then scooted into the back seat of the car. I pulled out my phone and read the series of worried messages. I felt so tired, and yet giddy and light at the same time. I tried to focus on the sign above the door of the bar, but I couldn't make my eyes focus on it. I looked back down at the phone as his last message came through:

Ruth, please let me know you're okay.

David, I wrote back. Just that. And I waited a minute, trying to stop myself from what I knew I was going to do. *Don't do this,* I thought to myself. *Stop. Stop. Stop now.*

Then I wrote: *I got your email.* Then, a second later: *Can I still stay at your house if I think I might like you?* And then: *I wish you were here. You said you wished you were on the trip with us. I wish you were too.* Finally: *David, I really like you.*

The whole drive back to the Sleepy Inn Motel, as Kay and Diane chatted in the front seat about the death of agriculture in the Canadian west, I sent David one text after another, my eyes sometimes drifting closed for a moment, then popping open to send another message. He hadn't replied to any of them. Just before we pulled into the motel parking lot, I sent: *David. Do you like me at all?*

Diane parked the car in front of the motel office, and after thanks and good nights, Kay and I made our way along the front of the units until we reached ours.

"You going to be okay?" asked Kay.

I looked down at the phone in my hand. Still no answer. "Kay, can you call David from your phone and let him know you are home safe? He's worried," I said. I could hear myself slurring slightly. "Tell him I'm sorry for whatever I said."

Kay frowned and glanced down at my phone. "All right. Drink some water before you get into bed."

"I will," I promised. But a moment later, I was unlocking the door to my room, pulling off my shoes and crawling under the covers fully dressed.

I was just about to drift off when the phone, still in my hand, buzzed.

Mom called. I am glad you are both safe.

I stared at the screen, waiting for something else to follow, something *better*. The room spun a few more times and then, like a switch had been flipped, I was out.

20

Furry. Fuzzy and furry.

Those were the only words to describe it. My tongue was covered in layers of fuzzy fur. God, I was so thirsty. I sat up, tentatively, and squinted. The clock said it was ten in the morning. My head was pounding, my tummy was about to revolt, and my tongue was, as mentioned, furry. Fuzzy. Both.

A knock came at the door, and Kay called my name. Had she been standing out there trying to wake me for a while? Probably. I pulled myself out of the bed, unlocked the door, yanked it open, then turned immediately and lay back down.

"Good news," she said.

I grunted.

"Christ in his high chair, Ruthie; it stinks in here," Kay said.

I grunted again.

"Are you feeling okay?" she said, chuckling.

A third grunt. That was all she was getting from me.

"All right, well—like I said, good news," she paused, perhaps expecting another grunt, but I didn't even move. "Randy called this morning. His friend or cousin or whatever got the part out to him yesterday, and he worked on it till midnight. It's done. We can get back on the road."

Was she kidding? That wasn't good news. I needed at least a day to lie here and die.

"David will be pleased, I'm sure," said Kay.

David. Oh. Fuck. David. My hand scrambled through the sheets, looking for my phone. I reopened our text thread, reading back over the final hour of conversation from the night before.

I groaned. "Oh. Shit. Shit. Shit. Shit. Shit."

Kay waited.

"This is bad," I said, finally looking at her, my face hot.

"I'm sure it's not that bad, Ruthie; you really are your own worst enemy," she said.

For once, I didn't care about trying to save face, and I shoved the phone in her direction, my eyes challenging her. "It *is* that bad. Read it. I told him I liked him. I told him he was cute. I told him that I wished he was here."

"That's not so bad," said Kay, helpfully. "That's just … honest, right?"

"Kay."

"Well, it is honest. I've known for ages that you like him."

"But I didn't want *him* to know."

"Why not?"

"Because I'm barely over Jack-ass, and probably not actually over him at all, and now I just poured my heart out to someone, and he answered with 'I'm glad you're both safe.'" My head pounded with each word that came out of my mouth.

"You probably surprised him, is all. Wait and see. Also, you'd had a lot to drink, and it's obvious in the messages. If someone told you these things when they were drunk, you'd not be sure if they meant it either."

"Yeah, well, I meant it. Because I'm an idiot, I guess."

Kay sighed. "Randy is bringing the van over here in a half-hour. Diane said she'd make us some breakfast so we can get on our way. It's about four hours to Medicine Hat, so let's try to get that far, if you think you're up for it. I can drive too. And we'll worry about my idiot son later, okay?"

I looked up at Kay, her shape outlined by the bright light from the door, and I knew she was looking at me with something between sympathy and affection. She wasn't frustrated that I was being stupid or that I'd gotten so drunk in the first place. She was being patient and generous, and I suddenly needed to tell her about Bernie—that I'd found him, and that I had told him we were coming. "Kay, I have to tell you—" I started.

Just then, Diane appeared at the door with two plates of scrambled eggs and toast.

"Oh, smells great," said Kay.

My stomach did not agree. I bolted to the bathroom, where I stayed for the next hour, being sick.

＊

By three that afternoon, we were halfway to Medicine Hat. The engine was running smoothly, and Randy had also cleaned and vacuumed out the van, so it felt like we were in someone else's fancy new vehicle. We'd stopped for gas in Moose Jaw, and while I pumped the gas, Kay had bought a tourist magnet in the shop, adding it to the growing collection on the hood of the car.

"How are they still there?" I asked, as we drove along the highway a few miles shy of the Alberta border.

Kay looked up and through the windshield and shrugged. "Strong magnets don't have to be big. Just like people."

I snorted. "Oh, thank you, Voltaire. Any more philosophy and wisdom to impart?"

"No, that's it for now. I dispense my jewels one at a time. All right, this list is doing really well. I mean, we're about 75 percent to completion."

I glanced over as she ran her pencil down the sheet of paper. "What's remaining?"

Kay scanned the list. "Well, in no particular order: see the dinosaurs at Drumheller, watch a sunset or sunrise from a mountaintop in BC, read three Canadian authors while on the trip. I got sidetracked with the romance novels, but I'm midway through the second Canadian book."

"What was the first one?"

"Oh, I read *The Conjoined* before we'd even made it to Ontario," she said. "Right now, I'm midway through *Son of a Trickster*. And I'm not sure yet what my third one will be. Maybe poetry. I bet there's a book store or two in Banff where I could find something."

Banff. That assumed the Highway 1 route, and I was already plotting how to take the Highway 3 route. *Later*, I told myself again, *think about it later*. Later would have to be pretty damn soon—at Medicine Hat, we'd have two choices: northwest for Highway 1 through Calgary and then Banff and into BC, or southwest for Highway 3 through Lethbridge and then into the Crowsnest Pass and the Kootenays, stopping in Rossland and then on through Osoyoos. I'd spent some time looking at the map on my phone as I'd eaten a piece of plain toast before we'd started driving. Today was definitely the last day before I'd have to confess it somehow.

"Slow the car down," said Kay.

I was about to ask why, till I saw the sign: Welcome to Wild Rose Country. At each provincial border, we'd stopped so I could take a photo of Kay under the welcome signs. "This is our penultimate sign," said Kay, as she unbuckled.

"It's our *what*?"

"Penultimate. Means 'second to last'. We cross this border— it's our second to last—and then the BC border will be the final one, and of course there's the Continental Divide as we go through the Rockies, but that's not a border. So this is our penultimate welcome sign. It's a great word. It's not first or best; it's not last or most important, but it's extra special, in its own way."

She did, indeed, dispense her jewels a little at a time.

✳

We checked into a hotel in Medicine Hat at about seven that evening, stocked up on a few snack items from the little pantry shop next to the front desk, and gave each other a nod and a good night in the hallway. We were both exhausted and had agreed during the last few miles into town that, after check-in, we'd go our separate ways and crash. I'd gotten used to being with Kay all the time, though, and as tired as I was, it felt strange to be alone. I flipped the TV on and let the noise fill the room as I unzipped my bag and found my toiletries so I could go have a shower. I sat on the edge of the bed and took out my phone. I hadn't fully read through the texts I'd sent from the bar the night before and had tried to avoid thinking about them the entire drive, but now I couldn't resist. As I scrolled through, I could feel my face getting hot all over again. I sounded ridiculous. And very drunk. And he clearly wasn't interested at all. Maybe Kay had told him about Jack-ass, and that's why he'd offered to let me stay? He felt sorry for me, perhaps.

I went to the bathroom, stripped and took a quick shower, then returned to the bedside and started digging through my increasingly disorganized bag for a nightie. I finally spotted a flash of the material and yanked at it, pulling with it the sex toy that Kay had bought me—which I had rolled up inside this nightshirt and forgotten about.

It was still inside the box. I opened the top flap and pulled the packaging out. There was a little yellow Post-it Note with Kay's handwriting: *I put batteries in. Enjoy!*

Oh God. Batteries? I turned the thing over and realized there was an end cap that must screw off to insert the batteries, and next to that was a small button with a power symbol on it. Above the power button were two buttons next to each other, one marked with a + and the other with a -, which presumably turned it up and down like a volume button.

I glanced over at the door to be sure it was locked and then hit the power button. It buzzed in my hand. I hit the + sign, and the vibration increased. I hit it a few more times, and the vibration went up each time till it maxed out at virtual earthquake level. I turned the power button back off and then lay down on the bed with my towel still wrapped around me. I felt self-conscious and foolish, but I let my mind wander to dancing with the guy at the bar the night before, how his body had felt next to mine, and how I'd felt imagining it was David instead.

I squeezed my thighs together and felt a small pulsing sensation between my legs. It had been so long since I'd had sex, and ages longer since I'd had good sex. Being intimate with Jack had started out all right, but over the years it had gotten repetitive—a sort of familiarity I'd assumed must happen in most long-term relationships. Sometimes I had an orgasm, if I paid careful attention to what was going on and moved in a very particular way, but most of the time I'd just smile at him after and say "almost" and "maybe next time." If he expressed any concern over this, I'd just say, "It's okay, I love that you're happy." As though his orgasm was the only one that counted, and mine didn't matter enough for either of us to work very hard for it. I'd spent the last few months loathing him for this lack of consideration—but thinking about it now, I realized I'd never once suggested it was a problem, or even implied that I wanted anything else. I had made him happy and feigned happiness in that. If his psychic-friends network didn't clue him in to the fact that the satisfaction wasn't running both ways, was that his fault or mine?

I imagined what it would be like to do those things with David, how different it might be. Would he be as formal in bed as he could be in text? The idea made me smile, imagining him asking politely if he might, for example, *perform a smidgen of oral sex on me.* Why I thought he'd say "smidgen" was beyond me, but the idea was comical all the same. And, actually, exciting.

I let my legs fall open just slightly, and then pushed the power button again on the toy. It buzzed to life in my hand and I moved it slowly down until it was just over the juncture of my thighs.

I squeezed my eyes shut and thought about David moving down the bed and kneeling there in the same spot, looking at me, licking his lips. The thought made my stomach do somersaults, and my hips curled.

I lowered the toy until I felt it touch me, the vibration unfamiliar but exciting. I pushed the + button and pressed the toy more firmly against me.

It was David's head between my legs, not my own hand and this battery-operated toy, and it was only a few seconds before the image of it, combined with the buzzing of the toy, had me nearly at the edge.

"Ohh. Ohh, ohh," I could hear myself making small breathy noises. "Dav—"

My phone rang. The screen flashed an incoming caller ID: David March.

"Jesus!" I scrambled to find the power button and couldn't. The phone rang a second time, then a third, and finally I gave up trying to shut the toy off. "Hi. Hello. Hi … can you hold on a second, just hold on a minute, one second, hold on. Okay?"

I set the phone down, grabbed the toy from where it was thumping about on the bed and tried to focus on it to find the button—why had it been so obvious before and now it was invisible? Was this some kind of special spy vibrator? What the hell? After what seemed like an hour, I figured it out, pressed the power button and turned it off, then retrieved the phone.

"Sorry about that," I said.

"Everything okay?"

"Yes, great. I was just … shaving my legs. So I needed to turn off the razor thingy, the machine thing, the shaver thingamajig. You know."

"Oh, I see."

I didn't respond, and I tried to control my breathing.

"Ruth, I just wanted to call and check in."

"Oh, yes, thanks. Everything is great. We got the van back earlier than expected, and we're in Medicine Hat, actually, so that's great."

"Oh, that's good news. I've been worried you guys might get a surprise snowfall coming through the mountains. It's a bit early for it, but it happens sometimes."

"Well, we'll keep our fingers crossed and hope for the best."

"Yes."

I wasn't sure what to say then, so I just stayed quiet.

Finally, he cleared his throat. "Also, I'm sorry I didn't answer your messages last night."

"Oh. That. It's fine. I was ridiculous and drunk and—"

"So it was just the alcohol talking."

"Yes," I said, voice resolute and firm.

"Oh, okay."

Silence for a moment. Panic fluttered through my chest. "Well, I mean … no. Yes, it was the alcohol talking in the sense that I wouldn't have had the bravery to say that stuff normally."

"But …?" he asked.

"But umm yeah, I guess I have thought … some of that … the things I said … before … I mean, I think about … well, it's just that … I'm not really saying it properly …."

"Ruth."

"Yes?"

"Yes, I like you. Too. Also, I mean. I also like you, a lot. And you are still welcome to stay here."

I opened my mouth, then closed it again. "Oh. Okay." I wanted to say: Oh my gosh, I like you and you like me, and I want to kiss you, and I'm really excited to see you and really scared too, and what does this all mean? Instead, I said: "Thank you, David."

It was his turn to be quiet now, and after a moment he cleared his throat and then spoke again. "Well, I imagine you must be really tired, so I'll let you sleep, okay? We can talk more … later?"

"David, I'm sorry about being drunk; I know it seems irresponsible, and I'm really sorry," I said all in a rush, wanting him to understand.

"Oh, my mom told me that she corralled you into going," he said. "Anyway, I'm not opposed to anyone having a good time, as boring as I may seem."

"I don't think you're boring at all."

He didn't say anything for a moment. "Okay, we'll talk tomorrow, then?"

"Yes, please," I replied, and it felt like we'd made a date, not just agreed to check in like we usually did, about where Kay and I were staying for the night and how the day had gone, but a *date* to visit with each other.

"Okay, tomorrow."

"Good night," I said.

"Good night, Ruth."

The phone went dead then, and I held it in my hand a second, thinking about the way his voice had sounded when he said, "I also like you, a lot"—like he was nervous that he might not get it all out if he didn't go fast. I lay on the bed a moment, feeling breathless and excited, then set the phone down again and grabbed the turquoise "doesn't look at all like a penis but is supposed to be a penis" vibrating toy.

I closed my eyes and let myself think of David, and his strange silver-grey eyes, and his formal funny personality, and his invitation to stay, and it did not take very long at all to imagine him leaning over me again.

21

INSPIRATION CAME ON the morning news. I flipped on the TV when I woke, and I listened half-heartedly while brushing my teeth. "Avalanche on Highway 1 a few kilometres west of Banff," I heard the newscaster say. "Crews are on site now, but the highway will be closed in both directions for at least the day. Police recommend detouring on …."

I zoned out on the rest of the information. We weren't scheduled to be through there for a day or two—in fact, we were going to deviate north to visit Drumheller first—but I could use this information as a reason to divert our course.

I opened the map on my phone and scanned the route. Fort MacLeod was about three hours away, and just beyond it was Head-Smashed-In Buffalo Jump. I knew what it was, but I did a quick google and discovered it was a UNESCO World Heritage Site. Surely that would be as compelling as Drumheller?

I met Kay in the lobby, and we walked out to the van side by side, loading our bags into the back. We'd become pros at this day-to-day packing and unpacking thing.

"Hey, tonight can we play some more crib?"

"Sure," said Kay. "That would be great."

When we got to the main intersection in town, with signs indicating one way for Route 1 and another way for Route 3, I was relieved that Kay was looking down at some paperwork in her lap, not paying attention in the slightest. I turned for Route 3 and wondered how long it would take for her to notice.

✳

Ten minutes, it turned out. It took ten minutes, precisely, for her to ask where we were and why the sign had indicated the distance to Lethbridge, not Calgary.

"Oh, well," I started. "Well."

"We're on the wrong highway, Ruthie," Kay said, unfolding her big map. "We need to figure out how to get back onto Highway 1."

"No, I changed my mind about the route," I said. "There was an avalanche near Banff, so we can't get through."

"But we won't even be there for a few days; we can go to Drumheller as planned, stop in Banff for a night. There's no rush," she said, as though it was the most logical thing in the world.

And it was, of course. It made more sense than diverting entirely. "Well, I saw on the map that Head-Smashed-In Buffalo Jump is along this route, and I thought you'd like that more than Drumheller. It's a World Heritage Site, you know. It's supposed to be really amazing. Also, you said you wanted to see the sunset or the sunrise on a mountain in BC, and it seems like the Kootenays would be a better place to do that, right?"

Kay looked at me like I'd gone mad. "No. I want to go to Drumheller. I booked a *tour* there, Ruthie. And I want to go to Banff. Highway 1."

I bit my lip. "No."

"Ruthie."

"No."

"Have you gone insane?" she asked, staring at me.

I refused to look away from the road. "No. I've just decided that we're taking Highway 3, that's all. And David said I'm in charge, so—"

"Oh, is that so? David is in charge of you, and you're in charge of me. And I'm the oldest one here, and everyone is going to treat me like a child who doesn't know how to do anything."

"No, it's not like that."

"Ruthie, turn the car around. We're going to Drumheller."

"No."

"Turn the car around."

"No!"

"Turn the goddamn car—"

"I can't! Okay? I can't. We have to be in Rossland tomorrow."

"What?" Kay shook her head. "Why?"

I hesitated. Why had it seemed like a good idea to do this secretly? What had I been thinking? "Because … because I found Bernie. In Rossland. And he's expecting us."

For the next sixty seconds, the only sound was the hum of the engine and Kay's fast breathing. Fuck. I had really messed this up. It was supposed to be a fun announcement, something exciting and great I'd done for her.

When she finally spoke, her voice was ice and steel. "Stop the car."

"What—"

"Stop the car."

"I can't—"

"Stop the car, Ruthie," Kay yelled. "Right the goddamn now!"

I pulled over to the shoulder as far as possible and let the car slow as dust swirled up around us. She pulled open her door and got out, walking back the way we had come. I watched her in the rear-view mirror and waited for her to stop. When she had gone fifty metres, then a hundred, then two hundred without slowing, I finally hopped out of the car and followed.

"Kay," I yelled. "Stop. Please."

She kept on as though she couldn't hear me. "Kay!" Still nothing. I picked up my pace to try to catch up. "I thought you'd be excited. I thought you'd want to see him again."

She stopped and turned around. Her face was streaked with tears. She stared at me and waited as I approached, my steps slowing as I got closer.

"Don't you want to see him again?" I asked tentatively.

She opened her mouth, hesitated, then spoke: "I left him without any word or explanation. I don't know why he'd even want to talk to me again."

"Well, he does. I've been emailing with him, and he invited us to come."

She blinked. "He knows I'm coming?"

"Yes, that's what I said in the car. He knows we're coming. We're expected. He *wants* to see you, Kay."

She shook her head, like it was an impossible idea. "You don't understand."

"Tell me."

"You won't like it," she said.

"It has nothing to do with me," I replied. "Tell me."

"Fine. Are you ready, Ruthie? I didn't *date* Bernie before I met Bill. He was *already* married to Sophia. I was *already* married to Bill. We had an affair, and I loved him more than there are words to describe, and when it ended, I didn't tell him where I was going, or why, or anything at all. I just disappeared one day. I left him, and I have no doubt he has hated me for it every day since."

I opened my mouth, then closed it again. Kay had cheated on her husband, on David's father. Kay and Bernie had not been a couple; they had been a secret. Kay was Jack. I turned around and started to walk back to the van.

"I don't know what possessed you to do this," she yelled.

I kept walking.

"It was none of your business," she shouted.

My stomach hurt. No wonder Kay had been all "grey area" when the topic of Jack's infidelity had come up—because she was as guilty as he was. I spun around and pointed my finger at her. All the calmness I'd begun to feel about Jack, the responsibility and ownership I'd begun to take for my part in our failed relationship, suddenly disappeared, a strange mix of embarrassment and betrayal replacing it. "How could you let me go on and on about Jack and all of that, knowing … this."

"It's not the same thing," she said.

"It's not? It is *exactly* the same thing, Kay. In fact, it's probably worse in your case. You were actually married."

"Christ almighty. You're so … so rigid, so black and white on every single thing. You have no idea what you're talking about. Bill was away all the time, and Bernie's wife was … it was very complicated. Goddammit. Why am I explaining this to you?"

I turned again and continued back to the van. I could hear Kay walking behind me, keeping pace.

"So we're going to Drumheller, then," she said.

"Nope."

"Ruthie!"

"I told Bernie we were coming, and I'm not going to disappoint him now. He thinks you're excited about it," I said, my voice flat.

"So you lied to me and you lied to Bernie, but you're the wounded party here because somehow what I did before you were even born is just, what? Salt to the wound of what Jack did to you? The world doesn't revolve around you, Ruthie, and not everyone who does a bad thing is a bad person. This way of looking at the world, like everyone who makes mistakes is terrible and unredeemable —it's going to make you lonely and scared and angry for the rest of your life."

I kept walking.

"Ruthie," she called again.

I didn't slow my pace at all. When I reached the van, I got in, did up my seat belt, started the engine and waited. I could wait here all day in silence if necessary.

Kay reached her side of the van and looked at me through the window, then opened the door and got in.

For a split second, I considered turning around and heading toward Drumheller after all. But I started the car and pulled back out on the highway, due west. My plotting until now had been a complicated but organized weaving, but it had suddenly become a tangle. Undoing these knots seemed more impossible than carrying on, and I didn't know what else to do anyway.

✳

Eight hours later, we still hadn't spoken a word to each other, and we'd stopped for a visit at Head-Smashed-In Buffalo Jump, had a quick lunch at a gas station, and then found a small motel just over the BC border in the town of Sparwood.

As we unlocked the doors to our rooms next to each other, I said: "We'll be heading out at eight in the morning, and that should get us to Rossland by two, including rest stops."

Kay opened her mouth to respond, but I pushed open my door and went through it as fast as I could. As I turned the deadbolt on the other side, it dawned on me how ridiculous it was that I was telling Kay who she was going to see and when, but I'd dug myself into it this far, and if I was being honest, I really didn't want to disappoint Bernie. He seemed a very sweet sort—though I supposed, when I thought about it, that he had been like Jack too, cheating on his wife—whatever the "complicated" reason was.

I threw my bags on the armchair and lay down on the bed. I was getting tired of having limited places to sit, eating cross-legged in the middle of the bed, and opening a new bar of soap in a new bathroom every day. What had seemed fun and exciting at the beginning had become repetitive, dull and depressing. I opened my phone and brought up the text thread with David. May as well let him know about the change of plans too—or at least whatever deceitful version I was willing to offer him. I refused to think about the irony of railing at Kay about honesty while I pecked away yet another lie to David.

Hi. Just wanted to let you know we've diverted a little bit. Long story (partly the result of an avalanche on Highway 1 near Banff), but we're now on Highway 3. We're in Sparwood tonight.

It took only a second for him to reply. *That means we're in the same province now.*

Yes, that's true. But different time zones. We're still on Alberta time here.

Really? I didn't know that.

Yep, we cross into Pacific time tomorrow. I think we'll be stopping in Rossland tomorrow night.

So then maybe just a few more days till you arrive?

I guess so, yes.

I'm really looking forward to it.

I thought about the fact that I hadn't spoken to Kay all day and realized the previously cozy notion of staying with David after we arrived might be out the window. But there was no way to explain that. It made me feel even lonelier.

Yes, me too.

Maybe we can all go out for dinner to celebrate, after you get here. The next day, after you've rested up.

Yes, that might be nice.

But everything is okay there otherwise?

Yes. Good night.

22

A s HAD BECOME our habit, I met Kay in the lobby, both of us carting our own bags. I barely looked at her, then went to the front counter to check out. With the keys dropped off and the bill paid, I headed out to the parking lot, assuming Kay would follow, but not waiting to see or even to acknowledge her. We loaded our bags into the back of the van, climbed into our seats and buckled in; it felt like we'd done this a million times, not just a dozen.

We drove in total silence for two hours, and then we both saw it at the same time: the first sign for Rossland and the distance to it. Kay tensed in the seat beside me, and I noticed her flick her hand at a bit of lint on her leg. She cleared her throat. "Do I look all right? I mean, do I look very … do I look okay?"

I glanced over at her, and for a second, the anxiousness on her face made me soften. I knew exactly what she was doing: she was imagining how much she'd aged since she'd seen Bernie last—or, more accurately, since Bernie had last seen her. "You look great. Really."

"Thank you."

But when she tried to make eye contact with me, I turned my eyes back to the road and pretended not to notice. I wasn't ready to be her friend again.

✳

We pulled into Rossland right on schedule, and I found the small hotel I'd located on Google the night before. We were scheduled to meet Bernie at three, at a coffee shop around the corner from the hotel. I explained this to Kay in a flat tone as we got our bags out of the car and checked in.

"We can walk there," I told her. "I'll just meet you out here in forty-five minutes, okay?" It was absurd of me to assume I was part of this, as though I needed to walk Kay to the coffee shop like she was a child going to school, but if Kay thought the same thing, she didn't say so. She nodded and followed me down the hall to our rooms. Once I'd dropped my bags, I checked my phone for the hundredth time—no reply from Jules, still, and just one from David, asking me to check in when we were settled for the day.

I sent him a quick text, telling him the name of the hotel. He replied, asking if we knew where we might stop tomorrow.

Probably Osoyoos. Seems like a good drive from here to there.

Yes, it would be, assuming the weather is good. From Osoyoos into Vancouver is only maybe five hours or so. You could be here in two nights.

Might be, yes. Hard to believe we're almost there.

What would you like for dinner when you arrive? I'll make sure I have all the ingredients ready. I'm sure you're done with hotel food.

I hesitated, fingertip hovering above the screen. *Maybe something West Coast. Salmon?*

Yes, I can do that. I'll BBQ it outside, cedar plank. And asparagus? Salad?

That sounds great. I'd love that.

I was letting myself forget the whole issue of "not speaking to Kay" while I enjoyed the fantasy of eating dinner at David's house. It was like play-acting, a pretend version of me who still knew what was going to happen tomorrow.

Have to get going. Kay and I are going to go for a walk around town.

Okay, be safe. Come back later to talk more, if you can.

I will, for sure.

It's a date :)
I grinned, letting myself pretend all was well.

✳

Kay was waiting by the door. She'd changed into a new outfit, and she'd obviously put on a bit of makeup and fixed her hair. She looked gorgeous, frankly, the kind of "old lady" I always hoped I'd be someday: casual but classy, graceful and calm. She looked … regal. She was holding her head high, her chin up slightly. She looked excited, and also terrified. The purple-silver hair was stylish perfection. I wanted to tell her everything would be okay, but I couldn't get the words out. They were stuck in my mouth, jumbled up with anger about Jack and change and choice and not having the life I'd imagined. All my kindness had disappeared, somewhere between the person I was a year ago—even the person I was yesterday—and the one I was today. "Well, let's go," I said.

It hadn't occurred to me till just then that Bernie would discover that Kay hadn't known about the plan all along, and he'd also realize I'd lied, but it was too late to come up with a plan—and anyway, being sneaky had worked out terribly this far. We walked in silence up the small-town street, both of us pretending to be interested in the various storefronts, peering in windows as we passed them. We got to the corner and turned left, and I spotted the Cozy Coffee Café on the other side of the street, about four doors up.

I could feel the vibrations coming off Kay as she stood next to me. She was totally still but poised to run—like a gazelle in a nature documentary, about to be chased by a leopard.

"Oh," she said, more breath than word, and I followed her eyes across the street. A man had stepped out of the coffee shop and was looking in our direction. He put his hand over his eyes against the bright sun, to get a better look, and then he raised the other hand in greeting.

Kay gasped, then took a big breath and blew it out slowly. The man smiled, his grin so big and bright that I thought he might start laughing. Kay smiled and then raised her hand in return. The man scanned for cars, then stepped off the sidewalk and all but sprinted, diagonally, to where we stood. Kay still hadn't lowered her hand, and from where I stood a few feet away, I could tell she was starting to cry, even though she was still beaming.

When he reached our side of the street, Bernie stepped up onto the sidewalk and slowed just slightly, opening his arms as he approached her—giving her a chance to indicate if she wasn't comfortable with a hug. But she stepped forward, finally moving, stepping into the circle of his arms, letting him wrap himself around her.

"Katie-Kay, my Katie-Kay, is it you? It's really you; I can't believe it." He squeezed her so tight that had it not been for the different colours of their clothing, it would be hard to tell where he ended and she began. I could see his hands gripping at her back, his fingers pressing into her through her blouse, as she began to cry in earnest, her shoulders moving up and down quickly as she sobbed soundlessly.

"It's okay. Katie, Katie-Kay, it's okay, it's okay," he said, soothing and calming her.

She said something into his shoulder, muffled, and it sounded like, "I'm sorry," but I wasn't sure until I heard him say in reply: "No sorry, no sorry. You're here now. It's okay."

He loosened his grip on her a little then, enough to turn his head toward me. "Ruth?"

"Yes," I said, barely a whisper.

"Thank you. Thank you for finding me."

I smiled a half smile and shrugged, as though to say no problem. I didn't know whether to feel angry or sad or happy, so I didn't say anything at all.

Kay pulled back from him a little, looking up at his face. "You haven't changed at all," she said, amazement in her voice.

Bernie laughed. "Then you need glasses, love. I'm a wrinkled-up prune; you just can't tell because you're crying."

Kay laughed, a hiccupping sort of noise that was half cry, then burrowed herself back into his chest. A moment later, she was sobbing in earnest again, and he was shushing her with quiet words.

I'd begun to feel like a voyeur, watching something I wasn't supposed to. "I'm going to ... okay, well, you guys catch up; I'm going to go back to the hotel or ... something," I said.

Kay didn't even hear me, but Bernie looked my way, smiled and nodded, his expression full of gratitude, like I was his guardian angel.

"My truck's up here," he said to Kay. "Let's go for a drive, okay?"

He put his arm around Kay, and they began to walk up the sidewalk away from me. I watched as he guided Kay to her door and helped her in. He leaned over her and kissed her forehead before closing the door, and then he walked around to his side. The whole time, Kay's eyes tracked him, watching him, making sure he didn't disappear, and when he got to his side and opened the door, she shifted sideways toward him as far as the seat belt would allow. He looked at her, smiled, then started the truck and pulled away, giving me a quick salute as he passed.

I stood on the sidewalk for another minute, unsure where to go next or what to do with myself. I looked over at the coffee shop we'd planned to meet at. A coffee seemed as good an idea as any.

❋

I didn't hear from Kay for the rest of that day, overnight, or the next morning, and by noon—after I'd called her phone a few times already with no answer—I'd begun to panic a little bit. I was avoiding David's texts completely, other than a quick note to let him know that we'd be staying in Rossland another day, as Kay wanted to "explore and sightsee" a little.

I'd started to imagine that maybe Bernie was actually a serial killer who'd taken her off to some mountain cabin and hacked her to pieces. Or that they'd had a car accident, and no one knew to call me to let me know. Anything was possible.

I paced the hotel room, then paced from the room to the lobby, and then started to walk along the street in front of the building. At three, I realized I was starving and needed to eat something, so I went back to the room to get my purse.

I was zipping up my jacket and getting ready to leave again, purse in hand, when I heard a noise in the room next door. "Kay?" I said, my heart racing.

I unlocked the chain on my side of the door and turned the knob, but the lock on the other side must have still been turned over, so it wouldn't budge. I knocked hard and shouted her name. The noise on the other side of the wall quieted, then the lock clicked, and the door swung open.

"Look, Ruthie, you've said your piece, and I understand where you're coming from, but I don't really want another round of your lectures," she said, looking slightly to the side of my head, as though she was refusing to make eye contact.

"Well, I just—"

"No. I'm not joking. Look, I'm getting my things, and I'm going to check out and spend a few days at Bernie's," she said, turning back to her bed, where her suitcase was laid out, clothes piled around it.

"David will—"

"I don't give a single fig what David thinks about it. I don't give a fig what you think about it. The pair of you think you know everything about everything, and everyone ought to do things the way you would do them. Look, you said once that you would never do what Jack did, and—"

"I wouldn't—" I interjected, but she put her hand up.

"And that may well be true, but you don't know the first thing about my life or Bernie's. We had our reasons."

"Did Bill even know about—"

She shook her head, folding another sweater and putting in the suitcase.

"No, he did not. It would have been no benefit for him to know. It was a different time, Ruthie, a totally different world than today. People didn't just ... get divorced. Bill and I were stuck with each other, whether we wanted to be or not," she said. She sighed, something between anger and exhaustion, and sat down on the bed. "Bill and I dated in high school, *casually*. Then we went on and dated other people. I heard through the grapevine that he'd fallen in love with a girl at university. His parents disapproved of her because she was Catholic, and they more or less sabotaged it. He was home over Christmas, and a group of us went dancing. I invited him along. We had a lot to drink, and ...," she shrugged. "When our parents found out I was pregnant, they made us get married. We liked each other well enough, but we weren't in love, not then— over time, we did grow to love each other very much. But neither of us wanted to marry the other, not deep down. And then we lost the baby, when I was seven months pregnant, and by then it was too late to undo everything." She paused a moment, closed her eyes and took a deep breath. "When we moved to Ottawa, Bill spent a lot of time travelling, for work. I never asked, but I was pretty sure he went to see his old girlfriend too, the one his parents disapproved of. And I was okay with that. I understood that."

"What about Bernie's wife?" I asked, quietly. "Did she know? Did she find out? Did Bernie even love her?" They were selfish questions: I didn't care about Bernie's wife, not really, but she was my foil in this story.

"That's not really my story to tell, Ruthie. But he had his reasons too," she said. "No one planned any of this. It just happened."

It just happened. I hated that reason. It absolved everyone of responsibility.

"Is David ... is David even Bill's son?" I asked. "Did you keep that a secret too?"

"David arrived several years *after* Bill and I had returned to PEI—and thank God for him," Kay said, her eyes closing. "Without David, I'm not sure what would have become of us. He made us a family, and it worked, for a really long time. It worked until Melissa died, and until Bill died, and really nothing has worked since then at all."

"I just think you—" I started.

She cut me off again. "Look, I've already told you more than you deserve to know. Hard as it may be to believe this, I don't require your approval, Ruthie. I would like your friendship, but I sure as hell don't need your permission to have lived my life up till this point." She closed the suitcase and picked it up.

"What am I supposed to tell David?" I asked.

"Make something up. You've gotten very good at that lately." She walked to the door, nodded without turning all the way around, and was gone.

23

I SPENT THE NEXT three days trying to avoid David's texts and calls. I told him that Kay had insisted we stay a few days to rest and sightsee, and I continued to check in with random details, like we'd gone for a hike on nearby Red Mountain, found some local hot springs, went for a spa day and did some shopping.

None of it was true, of course. I hadn't seen or heard from Kay at all, and every hour that passed, I became less convinced that I *would* hear from her. Maybe she was just going to move in with Bernie and call it a day?

I spent my time doing nothing and everything, trying to fill the hours, keeping my phone close by in case Kay called. I went to the library and spent an afternoon reading Susan Musgrave poems. One of them was about two couples out for dinner, and the narrator and the man from the other couple were having an affair— their hands and knees and legs touching under the table. It was full of fire and heat and very little guilt. Was everyone bound and determined to hurt the people they were supposed to love? I wandered the main street and went for coffee and took all my clothes to the laundromat to wash everything. I went swimming at the hotel pool two or three times each day, and at night I walked up to the café to buy a sandwich for dinner.

It was beautiful here; I could see why Bernie had chosen this place. It was cold and crisp, and every morning I was surprised that it hadn't snowed overnight. The mountains were gorgeous, covered in evergreens, lush and wild and overgrown, touches of white near the tops. Soon everything would be covered by snow, a lacy white dress for the hillsides.

Kay could go up to Red Mountain, the nearby ski hill, and watch the sun set or rise. She'd be happy with that, to be able to check another item off her list.

I laughed suddenly, realizing that chances were good she'd crossed off our most heavily discussed item, #20—and probably a few times at that.

I smiled, happy for her. And then I frowned, uncertain again. But I wasn't really mad at her, was I? It hadn't been my business to be mad over this in the first place. I was embarrassed for what had happened to me with Jack, and increasingly ashamed of my own part in all of it—the way I had insisted on the way things "ought to be" in our relationship and ignored entirely that our connection had been failing from not too long after it began.

But right now, all I could feel was sadness, a strange sort of envy. Had anyone ever loved me as much as Bernie loved Kay? Had anyone needed me as much as Kay had needed Bernie on that sidewalk? Had anyone touched me as tenderly, as carefully as Bernie had touched Kay, or looked at me as though I made the world perfect just by existing in it, as Bernie had looked at Kay?

Nope. No one. Ever. Definitely not. And I couldn't imagine that anyone ever would.

✳

I'd just finished eating my dinner at the coffee shop (yet another sandwich and side of coleslaw) when my phone rang. I looked at the screen: it was a number I didn't recognize, but I knew it was the local area code. The hotel, maybe?

"Hello?"

"Ruth, it's Bernie. Where are you?"

He sounded hushed, and his words were coming out fast.

Something was wrong. *Fuck.* "At the café. What's wrong?"

"Kay took a spill, sort of. She's hurt quite badly," he said. "We're at the ER, but they're admitting her. They want to run more tests, and her leg may be broken, and her blood sugar is really low, and—"

"I'm coming." I hung up and ran out of the cafe, then realized I had no idea where the hospital was and ran back in to ask the cashier.

"Trail," she said.

"Which trail?"

"No, no, that's the name of the town. Get back on the highway, about fifteen minutes up the road, heading east."

It was the first time I'd been in the van in nearly a week, and I realized with a pang that I missed it, getting in and driving to some new place every day. It smelled as it always did—like coffee, and dust from the boxes in the back, and the last bit of fragrance from the car freshener tree hanging in the rear.

I pulled out of the hotel parking lot and onto the highway. Oh God, I had failed at the one and only thing I'd been tasked with doing—keeping Kay safe. There was no way to avoid telling David this. Kay was in the hospital, I hadn't seen her in days, and I didn't even know what was wrong with her.

The traffic was slow as molasses on a cold winter day, and I could feel my heart skipping so fast that it was making me breathe hard to keep up. I spotted the "H" sign, and I followed the arrow, then another one, and hoped I was going in the right direction. When I came around the last corner and spotted the Kootenay Boundary Regional Hospital, I almost cried.

"I'm looking for Kay March. She came in a while ago with—" I hesitated. "I'm not sure, maybe a broken leg. She was with a man. I'm her caregiver."

"Are you family?"

"No, but I'm travelling with her, and her family hired me to be her companion."

I had been neither caregiver or companion, or even friend, in days. My shoulders slumped, and tears filled my eyes.

"Hold on," she said. She pushed her chair back from the counter, stood up and disappeared into another room behind her. She came back a minute later.

"She's been admitted, and she's in the process of having X-rays and blood work done, so you can't really see her right now," the nurse said. "But she'll be on the second floor, north wing, when she's transferred after that's all done. You can wait up there if you want."

I nodded and dashed, guessing at the best route to navigate the maze of hallways. When the elevator opened on the second floor, north wing, the first thing I saw was Bernie. He was sitting on a couch at the end of the hall, staring straight ahead. I waved, but he didn't see me until I sat down next to him.

"Oh, Ruth, hi," he said.

"Is she okay?"

"Yeah, yes, I think so. But she's hurt and … well, I don't know. We called an ambulance, and then we went to the ER, and they started to look at her, and she fainted, and … well, anyway, she's off getting a bunch of tests done, and so we wait, I guess."

"I can't believe this," I said.

"I know, me too. I feel awful."

"I do too. I should have been, I don't know, more careful. I should have insisted she stay with me instead of you."

Bernie looked at me and gave a sad half smile. "I know you haven't known Kay for long, but do you really think you'd have been able to talk her into doing something she didn't want to do?"

I shook my head no. "I have to call her son," I said.

"Yes, you'd better."

I got up, wandered back down the hall to a quiet area and dialed David's number, praying this one time it would go to voicemail.

"Hello?"

No dice. "Hi, David. I'm just calling … um, well the thing is …."

"Is Mom okay?"

"Well, she's had a little accident. Maybe a broken leg, they said, but we're waiting to find out."

"A broken leg, Jesus! What was she doing?"

"Um, well, I'm not totally sure. I was … umm, well, the thing is that I wasn't with her just when it happened."

"Where were you?"

"At the hotel."

"Where was she?"

"I don't know."

"Ruth. I don't understand."

"I know, it's complicated but—"

"Okay, okay, look, she's in the hospital? What hospital? Where?"

"Kootenay Boundary Regional Hospital."

"I'm on my way."

"David—" But he'd already hung up. Fuck. Fucking fuck fuck. I got back to the couch, where Bernie was still sitting, just as a doctor arrived.

"Ms. March has informed me that I'm to provide updates to Bernard Kowalski and Ruthie MacInnes—I trust that's you two?"

Bernie and I nodded at the same time.

"All right, well the short and the long of it is that she has a broken ankle and a broken wrist. She's also probably a bit dehydrated, and her blood sugar was very low when she arrived, likely a result of not having eaten all day. I'd like to keep her a day or two, considering her age, to make sure the breaks are starting to heal properly and to keep her on IV fluids and get her back up to her usual self."

I stared at him. "Okay. So she's okay, then, yes? She'll be okay?"

"Yeah, she should be fine," said the doctor. He turned to Bernie. "I might suggest a little less … enthusiasm, in the romance department. And take breaks to eat and drink." He winked at Bernie and turned away.

I swivelled my head to look at Bernie. "How did she hurt herself, *exactly*."

He looked somewhere between proud and embarrassed, and he shrugged.

"Did you guys have some kind of, like, sex marathon, and she fell out of the bed?" I asked angrily.

"Well, we weren't in the bedroom at that point, but …," he said, trailing off.

"Kay's in the hospital because you guys went on a multi-day shag fest, and she didn't eat or drink enough, and then she fell down trying to replicate some page from the Kama Sutra? Yes? That's what we're talking about here?"

"It sounds quite bad when you say it like that."

"How am I ever going to explain this to David?"

"Well, I'm not sure if David has noticed—or you, for that matter—but Kay is not an invalid or a child. What she does with me and the Kama Sutra isn't really anyone else's business."

"All right. You can tell David that when he arrives."

"He's coming?"

"Well, that was what he said when I called."

"This'll be fun."

I stared at Bernie. "Fun. Yeah. That's exactly the word I was thinking of."

24

B Y PURE DUMB LUCK, I'd been down in the cafeteria getting a coffee when David arrived the next morning. I got as far as Kay's door when I heard his voice from the other side. It was somewhere between worried, frustrated and frantic, with a touch of mad on top.

"Oh shit," I said under my breath. He must have caught the first flight up here this morning. Was there even an airport here?

I sat down in a chair opposite Kay's door and sipped my coffee. Every once in a while, one or the other of them would speak a little louder, and I could make out a few words. She was obviously filling him in on the list, my part in finding Bernie, and the diversion of the last few days.

"Staying *with* him? In his house?" I heard David repeat, somewhere between baffled and worried. "Ruthie said you were sightseeing. And going to the spa."

Their low voices continued, and I couldn't make out a word of it despite straining to eavesdrop. Finally, I heard Kay sigh, her voice just loud enough now to make out the next bit. "Oh David, I know you worry, but no amount of worry will keep me alive. You can't control everything. You couldn't control anything that happened to Melissa either. Things happen, and you have to just deal with them as they come. It's not your job to save everyone."

My stomach was in knots as I heard his low voice responding to that, and then suddenly his voice was rising again, distressed.

A nurse walked by just then, opened the door a fraction and poked her head in to ask Kay if everything was okay. When Kay turned, she caught sight of me in the hallway, and her face went sad and her eyes soft.

✳

I thought back to the night before. We'd had a long visit, after she'd finally gotten settled in the ward and before the nurse had kicked me out for bedtime.

"Well," Kay had said, when she'd seen me come into her room. "I guess you're not very impressed with me, are you, Miss Ruthie?"

I shrugged. "It's not my job to be impressed with you or not. It was my job to keep you safe. I guess I'm not very impressed with myself," I said, biting my lip. "And also, I was an asshole to you. I lied and tricked you and went behind your back to find Bernie, thinking I knew better than you. And when you told me about everything, I said awful things, things that I didn't mean."

Kay had shifted in her bed and then grimaced, as the movement gave her obvious pain. "Thank you, Ruthie. I shouldn't have gone so long without talking to you. I was mad when I left the hotel, but it wasn't fair to leave you worrying and dealing with David, and I knew full well you'd be doing both."

I shrugged, as though to say, "Oh well, such is life."

"Look, Ruthie, I'm not leaving. I'm going to stay here. With Bernie. You probably figured that already. I'll be calling David tomorrow. He won't be happy, but … I'm not leaving."

"I don't think you'll need to call him; he said he's coming here," I said. "And for the record, I wouldn't leave either. If I had a Bernie, I mean. I'd stay right here too."

Kay gave me a half smile, soft and gentle. It was the first time in days that she'd looked at me that way, like she was forgiving me for my nonsense.

"There's a Bernie for you. I suspect he's closer than you imagine," she had said.

If she meant David, she'd obviously forgotten the fact that this whole hospital-injury-Bernie-fiasco was not exactly a job well done on my part. I'd be lucky to even get paid, let alone have a hot date for my next Christmas party.

"Maybe."

"So you told David I'm here?"

"Yes, but I didn't know many details. He said he was coming, and then he hung up on me."

"Sounds like David. Well, I guess we'll be having a visitor soon, then. I hope he arrives before I get discharged. He won't be able to yell very loud in a hospital."

Kay had laughed at that, and the sound of it made me laugh too.

✳

And she'd been right, hadn't she, I thought now, as I looked into the hospital room and the nurse stood in the door. He couldn't yell if he wanted to. For a split second, I caught sight of the edge of his shirt as he paced back and forth somewhere behind the door and out of my line of sight. It looked blue, crisp, like a button-up dress shirt. I looked down at my clothes. I'd barely changed from what I'd been in yesterday, and my hair was total bedhead. Maybe I could escape and pretend I'd gone to the hotel for a rest.

I was just about to stand up when the nurse pushed the door a bit wider, and David turned his head at the same moment, spotting me. There was a roar like a jet plane in my head, and my whole body went from warm to hot and back to cold, as he stared at me. I couldn't move at all, not even to wave hello or to smile or anything. He continued to stare at me for another ten seconds, which felt like ten thousand, and finally, when I didn't think I could keep his eye contact for one more moment, he stepped toward me.

I stood up. This was not at all how I'd imagined this moment. I'd pictured pulling into his driveway in Vancouver. It would be sunny but cool. We'd see a movement in the window of the house, and I'd know he'd seen us. We'd get out of the van, I'd stretch, and then he'd open the front door. Of course, he'd go to his mom first and give her a big hug, but while he was hugging her, he'd be looking at me, smiling. He'd be so glad I was there. He'd maybe hug his mom longer than he normally would because even though he was excited, he was a little nervous, too, like me, and wasn't sure if he should shake my hand or hug me or just ravish me right there on the spot.

None of that was happening now, and it wasn't David's fault or Kay's fault or Bernie's fault. It was my fault. Everything I had done had landed us right here.

David strode out of the room and stopped a few feet from me. He was taller than I'd imagined, and I had to look up at him, which made me feel even smaller and more ridiculous. I crossed my arms in front of my chest, without thinking, and I saw his eyes drop, noticing, picking up my defensive move. He rubbed his hands over his face, looking both sad and exhausted.

"As my mother intends to live here, and she has no need for additional escort to the coast, your services are no longer ...," he paused, as though searching for the right word, "required. I will send you an e-transfer for your wages to date. Please let me know if you have incurred any incidentals, and I will reimburse you immediately. Let me know how you would like to return home, and I will see to getting it booked."

He sighed, and I stared at him, opened my mouth to say something, then closed it again. He waited a fraction of a second, and later I would tell myself that it was because he was hoping I'd say something then—apologize or beg him to stay, maybe even fling myself into his arms—but I was frozen.

"Right, then," he said. "Good luck with everything, Ruth." His voice was blank, flat—not disappointed, not sad, not angry. Just

… nothing. Which was somehow worse than disappointed or sad or angry. I could fix the other things, but I didn't have any tools against "nothing."

He turned and walked down the hall away from me. I could feel his name on my tongue, and I tried to force it out, to shout after him, anything to stop him long enough to let my brain work so I could tell him *something*, but it just didn't come out. He got to the corner, rounded it and was gone.

I looked across the hall and through the open door of Kay's hospital room, and I realized she was watching me. She was frowning. Her hand was gripping at the blanket beside her. She shook her head slowly and looked down at her lap.

I couldn't bear to see her sadness, realizing that as much as I'd begun to fantasize about some hypothetical future that possibly involved David, she had probably begun to fantasize about a hypothetical future that involved me too. Having watched her son lose his wife and child, watched him mourn these last few years, had she pinned some hope for David's happiness on me, hoping that this trip would be tied up with a nice bow and a happy ending for him?

Yes, she had.

So I'd let everyone down. My parents, for being such a screw-up. My sister, for not living nearby to be a good aunt. Jules, by being a terrible friend. Even Jack, in a way, I had let down by refusing to see for so long that what we had wasn't any good. Now Kay, and worst of all, David.

At every turn, I'd thought of myself first and everyone else second. Even tracking down Bernie had been about me—about playing matchmaker and thinking how grateful Kay would be to me for it. And here I was, in the middle of nowhere, thousands of miles from home—not that I actually *had* a home—with no one. Alone. Again.

25

I wish I could say that I remembered very much of the next twenty-four hours, but I don't. I went from the hospital to the hotel, parked the van, walked up the main street to the local bar and took a seat at the counter.

I drank a glass of wine. Then a second. That old familiar feeling started to cozy up to me—a warm, soft-edged cocoon wrapping me up. I'd lived in this soft, wine-dulled space after Jack, refusing to think about anything, but thinking constantly all the same.

By the end of the second glass, it occurred to me that I was alone in a town where I didn't know anyone, and getting drunk here might not be the best idea. Getting drunk was a good idea, I corrected myself, but doing it here, alone, wasn't.

So I went around the other side of the building to the cold beer and wine store and found two bottles of red wine. I didn't even look at the labels. Just the price. Both were under ten dollars. Good enough for me.

I carried them back to my hotel room, waving cheerily at the front counter staff on my way past, buoyed by the wine in my system. In my room, I got one of the water glasses from the bathroom, twisted off the screw cap of the first bottle of wine and poured the glass full—then drank it all in three gulps.

How had I forgotten how lovely this was? This nowhereness of tipsy. It absolved me of responsibility for everything I'd done, and even of responsibility to do anything. I didn't need to pay bills, think about the future, wash my hair. There was just this: blissful, blank wine dreams.

I drank a second glass, slowly this time, and flipped on the TV. *Gone with the Wind* was playing, and Scarlett was in Frank's mercantile. (Was that the right name? I wondered fuzzily. Mercantile? Market? Store? Dry goods store. Yes, that was it.) I got into bed, pulled the blankets up, set the glass on the bedside table and let my fuzzy brain turn off as I watched the film.

At some point, I must have fallen asleep—or passed out. I woke with drool on my face, all the lights on, and Bonnie Blue falling off her horse. I hated this part—the final nail in the coffin for Rhett Butler, the thing that killed the last soft spot inside of him. Everything he loved had disappeared, died or turned its back on him. *Like me*, I thought groggily. But even as the thought came into my head, I knew it wasn't exactly like me. Rhett wasn't to blame for Bonnie falling, or for Scarlett being so clueless about Ashley Wilkes. But I was to blame for plenty.

I reached for the glass on the bedside table and found it empty, so I located the bottle on the bureau and poured another glass.

✳

Two days passed more or less in this manner: I watched TV, I ate a little bit, I drank wine. I went out once to go back to the liquor store for another two bottles. I woke up groggy and sweaty and sore, and then I started over. I just didn't want to think about anything.

On the third morning, I woke up with a jolt. There was a knock at the door, and another, louder. David? My tummy fluttered and my heart leaped, but I knew it was ridiculous. Anyway, I'd noticed an email come in late last night with an e-transfer for the payment. As far as he was concerned, our connection was over and done.

I felt like I was going to vomit and cry at the same time. The knock came again, and I resisted the urge to yell at whoever was there to just go the fuck away already. I stumbled to the door, half dressed, and looked through the peephole.

Oh. Bernie. I pulled the door open wide. "Hi," I said, and turned my back to him, heading back to the bed. I didn't even care what he was there for. I just wanted to wallow, and I didn't want anyone to interrupt me.

He followed me in, letting the door close softly behind him. "Ruthie," he said, firmly but gently.

I just grunted as I got back into the bed.

"Kay sent me."

I didn't respond.

"I'm here to take you home. My home, I mean," he said.

"I'm not going," I said, my voice dead and flat.

"Well, Kay says you are—and she says if you put up a fight, to remind you that this room is currently charging through David's credit card."

I sat up. I hadn't thought of that. Bernie chuckled.

"It's not funny," I said. I knew I was behaving like a surly toddler woken early from an afternoon nap, but I couldn't stop myself.

"I have a spare room, a fridge full of food, lots of coffee," he said. "And a shower."

I looked around the room, imagining it from his point of view. It probably reeked in here too. I hadn't showered in three days. Or brushed my hair. Had I even brushed my teeth or changed clothes? I frowned. I didn't want to go anywhere or see anyone. Couldn't I just stay here for free, forever?

"May I sit?" asked Bernie, motioning to the edge of the bed.

I nodded and felt the weight of his body at the edge of the mattress. It felt so much like my dad sitting on the edge of my bed when I was a teenager—coming to talk to me about some drama at school or a fight with my sister—that I caught my breath and felt tears coming up, my throat choking closed.

"Ruthie, I'd be honoured if you would come and stay with me.

With us. Kay misses you. And she's worried about you," he said, his voice quiet and gentle. "But it's up to you."

I started to cry, a slow, pathetic sob, my shoulders hitching up and down, gasping as my sobs picked up speed. My nose was running, and I kept sniffling. I was sure I looked disgusting. I felt disgusting. Everything hurt, like I'd been in a boxing match and then passed out on the floor. "I'm ... I'm ... I'm ... sorry," I hiccupped out between sobs.

"I know."

"I'm sorry I lied to you."

"I know."

"I'm sorry I lied to Kay."

"I know."

"And David."

"I know."

"I'm sorry. I'm really ... I'm ... really... sorry." I was getting out of control, my volume increasing as I worked my way through apologies, crying louder and more forcefully, tears dripping off my chin.

"I know, Ruthie."

He opened his arms a little, the smallest invitation for a hug. Bernie was solid and warm and safe—it didn't matter that my hair was matted, and my nose was dripping, and that I smelled like a brewery. He stroked my back. "Shh."

"Everything is messed up," I whispered. "I wish I could start over. And do it all better. Everything." I cried in his arms then, for what seemed like an hour, but it was probably just a few minutes. When my sniffling slowed, he squeezed me hard.

"Ruthie," he said, close to my ear. "Your story hasn't even begun yet. You think you're at the end. You haven't even gotten past the first chapter. Trust me." His voice was so calm and slow and deep, hypnotizing. It sounded like a sermon, like wisdom from a mountaintop.

I pulled back from him and looked at his face. His eyes were gentle and sad.

"Trust me, Ruthie. I know," he said.

I nodded and wiped my face with the back of my arm.

"It's up to you, but if you'd like to come, I can wait in the truck while you shower and pack."

I thought about it for a moment. It was time to figure out the next step, to sort out my plan—and doing that at Bernie's would be far better than doing it here, holed up in this hotel room indefinitely.

"I'd like that," I said.

"No rush," he answered, then left the room.

I found a set of clean clothes in the bag I'd brought back from the laundromat but never put back in my suitcase, and I went to the bathroom, closing the door behind me.

✳

Two hours later, I was at the kitchen table at Bernie's, a plate of toast in front of me. My favourite kind: sourdough, toasted a light brown, with a thin layer of melted butter. And on top of that, another thin layer of peanut butter. As I chewed the toast, Bernie filled my coffee cup again, then sat across from me.

"So, they're letting Kay out this afternoon; I'm going to go pick her up. She's right as rain, so nothing to worry about there. She'll be in that boot cast thing for a few weeks, and a brace on her wrist, but that's all right. You know Kay; she'll do just fine, I'm sure," Bernie chuckled.

I smiled at him, then shivered. I felt fragile and thin, like I'd lost weight and strength and couldn't trust my own body to hold me up properly.

"Why don't you take a nap after I go, and then we'll be back by the time you wake up?"

I nodded. It was easy to sink into Bernie's caretaking, to let him "dad" me for a little bit. Already there was a small voice in the back of my head reminding me that this was not my home, that I couldn't stay forever, and that whatever the next stage was going to be, I would be figuring it out solo. Solo. For maybe the first time, the idea made me as much hopeful as scared.

While I'd showered back at the hotel, Bernie had arranged with the front desk to have one of the staff—who, by chance, was Bernie's best friend's grandson, because that's how things always seem to go in a small town—follow him with the van, so that all of Kay's boxes and belongings, and my other items, would be at Bernie's and not left behind in the parking lot. The van had made a funny noise when it started, perhaps from sitting for so many days, and Bernie cocked his head and listened.

"I'll have to take a look at that," he said. Then he'd driven us both back to his house, the loud diesel engine of his Dodge Ram blotting out the need to talk, with the van following behind us. When we'd arrived, the young man who had driven the van told him not to worry about a return ride; he was at the end of his shift anyway, and the manager had told him just to go home after, as he lived nearby. They chatted for a minute about this and that, and then Bernie shook his hand, thanked him and walked me into his house.

He'd pointed me to the kitchen table and immediately started making coffee and toast.

＊

As I finished the first piece and realized how hungry I was, I quickly started on the second.

"Want some more?" he asked.

"Yes, please, maybe one more."

He got up and popped more bread in the toaster. "So, that's the plan. I'll get Kay, you take a nap. Maybe I'll make some spaghetti and meatballs for dinner, eh?"

"That sounds really good," I said.

"And no wine." He frowned at me and then winked.

"No wine," I agreed.

"You need a new coping mechanism, kiddo. I hike. Every time I have a problem, I go for a hike. I hike a lot," he said, grinning. "It's a lot more work than wine, but it doesn't make me want to barf later. I'll take you for one when you're feeling better."

I smiled at him. "I'd really like that, please."

We sat and drank our coffees without talking, and eventually he stood up and told me he'd be back with my bags in a moment. When he returned, I followed him upstairs to a small bedroom, which had a twin bed and a desk.

"Was this one of your kids' rooms?" I asked.

"I never had kids," he said.

"Oh." I don't know why I had assumed, except that most people did have kids at some point. I still figured I probably would, even though the likelihood was slim to none at this point.

"You're welcome to stay as long as you'd like," he said. The words echoed almost exactly what David had said to me just last week in his email.

"Thank you, I appreciate it."

"Well, I'm going to head out. I'll stop at the store before I go to the hospital," he said. "Have a rest. We'll see you later." Bernie walked back out, closing the door behind him as he went.

I sat on the edge of the bed, already feeling ready to lie down and crash. I was exhausted, bone-deep exhausted. I looked around the simple room, but I could barely keep my eyes open long enough to look at the art on the walls or the knick-knacks on the bureau. I put my bags on the floor and lay down on the bed, pulling up the small blanket that was folded at the foot of the bed. I needed a nap. And maybe later, depending on how my stomach felt, spaghetti and meatballs.

26

IN THE END, I missed the spaghetti and meatballs. And breakfast the next morning. And lunch too. I slept for twenty-four hours, so deep and solid that Kay told me later she'd come in to check on me in the morning and wondered for a split second if I was even breathing.

"You were solid as a rock, and I had a panic for a second, like maybe you'd gone to sleep still drunk."

We were sitting in the living room, Kay on the couch and me on the loveseat. Bernie was in the kitchen making popcorn, because I'd mentioned that *Gone with the Wind* had been on TV at the hotel, which sparked a conversation about our favourite movies. Bernie and I had both mentioned that we loved *Scrooged*, with Bill Murray, and Kay said she'd never seen it. It wasn't anywhere close to Christmas, but Bernie pulled it out of his DVD collection and insisted we should watch it for Kay's education.

I had to agree, of course, and then I suggested we make it a full movie night complete with blankets, popcorn and hot chocolate. Kay chuckled, but Bernie jumped on the idea; I got the feeling both of them were relieved that I wasn't dead or still on a booze binge, which was an odd and lovely feeling. It meant they didn't hate me for the things I'd messed up.

So we'd gathered up blankets and got the movie lined up and ready to go, and Bernie made the popcorn while we waited.

"Look what I found," Kay said.

The list. She unfolded it and laid it on her lap, then reached forward to the coffee table to grab a pen.

"We can check off a few more, you know," she said.

I laughed. "Yeah—#20, like a hundred times, right?"

"Maybe 150, 200 … who's counting?"

"Ugh," I groaned.

"You're just jealous," she said, chuckling.

"Um, yeah, actually, I totally am. The dolphin is great and all, but …."

Kay's eyes went wide, and she hooted in surprise. I loved making her laugh like that. Her pen swiped across the page as she checked off two or three things, then she held the list up and scanned it again. Bernie walked in with two big bowls of popcorn, handed one to me, and then sat next to Kay with the other.

"I wrote a poem while I was in the hospital. It was terrible, but I wrote it. And I plan to buy something from a local artist at the farmers' market in Trail, which I'm told is pretty great. We crossed the Continental Divide that last day when we drove here. We didn't stop, but I'm still counting it. There are only two things left: watch a sunrise or a sunset from a mountaintop in BC and put my toe in the Pacific Ocean."

Bernie leaned over and looked at the piece of paper. "Ah, this must be the list I've heard about," he said, scanning it. "You stole something? What did you steal?"

Kay and I started laughing at the same time, and the story came tumbling out. Then another and another, and I had them both laughing so hard, they were holding their stomachs as I replayed the conversation with David on the phone while Kay had wandered around the Dungeon, talking about ball gags. I'd been infuriated in the moment, but now it seemed hilarious, my temper a childish leftover that I no longer recognized.

Bernie took the list and read through it again. "Well, there's nothing for it, ladies; you have to finish it off."

Kay pointed at her foot and the massive plastic walking cast that encased her leg from toe to knee. "I don't think I'll be climbing any mountains to watch a sunset anytime soon—and I don't plan on getting as far as the Pacific for a little while yet, remember?" she said, leaning over to give him a kiss.

"Well, that's true. I'm going to keep you to myself here for a bit, but we'll get there eventually," he said. "It would have been fun for you to get them all done as part of the one trip, but it's the idea of the thing that's great, isn't it? Not the specifics."

I nodded, then shook my head. "Wait, no," I said. "The list was Kay's, but it sort of became mine too. I can watch a sunset on a mountaintop, and I can put my toe in the Pacific Ocean. I've come this far; I may as well make it all the way to the coast before I decide what to do, right?"

Kay smiled. "You can take the van. If you come back this way, great. If not, it's on its last legs anyway," she said.

"And I'll take you up to watch a sunset tomorrow morning if you want, Ruthie," said Bernie. "I've been hiking these hills for more than half my life; I know the best spots. We'll go to one where we can drive most of the way, so we're not wandering about in the dark," he added.

"I'd love that," I said.

Kay held up her can of Coke with a flourish and made a toast. "To the list." We followed suit, and a round of cheers ensued, followed by long swigs of soda.

"Maybe we should save *Scrooged* for another night. If we're getting up that early, we'd probably better go to bed soon," I said.

The pair nodded their agreement. "I won't argue with that," said Kay.

"Me neither," added Bernie, pinching Kay's rear end as she stood up.

"Hey, jeez, she's already broken; don't make it worse," I teased.

"Don't worry. Kid gloves. I waited forty years for her to come back; I'm not going to lose her now," said Bernie.

Kay smiled a little, but the comment pained her, I could see. We'd talked in the hospital about this: the joy of finding each other, but still being broken and traumatized by what had happened, by the years apart and the uncertainty.

"Love is a strange sort of magic," Kay had said that night. "You think that love makes you immune to hurt, but I think it's maybe just the opposite. It only opens you up to it, more than you were before. Even if love stays, even if it all works out for you, part of you always knows that you've made yourself vulnerable to losing it."

I could see the echo of those words in her face now, and Bernie reached out to take her hand and squeeze it, as though he could sense it too, somehow. Then he helped her navigate through the room with the boot on, and they headed toward the hall. Over his shoulder, Bernie said: "Okay, kiddo, be ready at 5:30 a.m. I'll have the coffee made."

"Yes, sir." I offered a salute, then grabbed my blanket and headed to the stairs. I heard their door click shut down the hall. It was a strange thing, to wish they'd not had all the heartache in the years between then and now, and also to know that if it had played out differently, David wouldn't even be alive. But then maybe something else would have happened—a car accident, cancer, anything at all. Maybe heartache was just unavoidable. Perhaps all you could really do was hope that it would be short-lived and tolerable, and that in the end, everything would sort out as it should, somehow.

27

IT'S HARD TO TELL the difference between 2:00 a.m. and 5:30 a.m. in the mountains in autumn. There's no more hint of light at 5:30 than there is in the middle of the night. When I looked out the window of the spare room, I could see stars, but I couldn't see where the sky ended and the mountains began, or even the back fence of Bernie's yard, for that matter.

I got dressed in several extra layers and then stumbled down the stairs to the kitchen. Bernie, as promised, was already up with coffee; he handed me a travel mug as I walked in.

"Two cream, three sugar, right?"

I nodded, incapable of speech. He grabbed a backpack from the table and headed to the door. I followed, pausing long enough to pull on my sneakers and my jacket. Bernie tossed me a toque from the basket inside the hall closet, and when it was on my head, he handed me mittens and a scarf too.

"It's cold out there. If you don't need 'em later, that's okay, but you should have 'em now."

I just nodded again. Whatever he said.

"All right, here we go—#17, watch a sunrise from the top of a mountain in BC," he said. I could tell he was pleased to be part of the project now. He grinned at me, opened the door and let me go out ahead of him to the waiting truck, which was already running to warm it up. Thin sheets of frost slipped down the front windshield.

I hopped in the passenger side and waited while Bernie scraped off the side windows and the back of the canopy. When he got in, his face was pink from the cold, and he pulled off his gloves to drive. It would be winter here before long.

"All set?" he asked, putting the truck in reverse.

"Yep," I said, finally breaking my silence.

"Ah, she *is* awake," he said and chuckled.

"Barely. Thank you for the coffee," I added, hoisting the travel mug.

"You're welcome."

We drove in silence all the way through town and out onto the highway. About ten minutes along, Bernie turned off the main route onto a smaller side road, which wound its way upwards.

"This is sort of the backside of the ski hill. There are a lot of service roads here. If we were going for a daytime hike, I'd park on the other side at the base and walk you up; it's a few hours and beautiful all the way. But I don't want us to be in the dark, and there's a route up here that'll take us to a great vantage point facing east, to see the sun. We'll just make it, I think."

The road continued to wind back and forth, switchback after switchback. Eventually the pavement ended, and Bernie turned onto a gravel road that was barely wide enough for his truck.

"What happens if someone comes in the other direction?" I asked.

"We back up," he said.

"Oh."

After a kilometre or two, the gravel road came to a dead end, and he pulled in next to a small hydro station ringed by a tall fence. Beyond it was forest, visible only where the truck's headlights pointed. Bernie turned off the engine, and we got out.

He hitched the backpack up on his shoulder, and we circled around the enclosure. I followed as closely as I could. There had been an almost imperceptible shift in the darkness: what had been black a few moments ago was a deep navy now, and I could see the outline of trees and, thank God, Bernie's back.

He handed me a small flashlight and suggested I point it down at the ground—the path would end in a moment, and we'd be going through the woods, where small fallen branches might trip us up. I did as instructed, and we carried on for a few minutes in silence until, suddenly, the trees disappeared, and we were in a clearing.

"Here we are," he said. He walked another twenty paces and then pulled the backpack off, unzipped it and took out a blanket, which he spread out on the ground. "The bottom is waterproof; it'll keep us from getting wet from the dew."

I sat down on the blanket next to him, criss-crossing my legs, and looked in the direction he pointed.

"Okay, the sun will rise there in about … eight more minutes," he said, checking his watch. "If there was no mountain range here, sunrise would happen a little earlier."

"Makes sense," I said, and took a sip of my coffee, which I'd carried with me from the car in one hand, the flashlight in the other. We sat in silence for a moment, and then Bernie started talking.

"Ruthie, I'm grateful you found me. I know you feel bad that it was secret, and you tricked Kay, but she's forgiven you of course—you know that, right?"

I shrugged, though I wasn't sure he could see it in the dark.

"I know you think we did something awful, back then. And by rights, we did."

He was silent again. I could see the slightest lightening at the tip of the mountain range across from us, a glimmer at the edges of the rocky terrain.

"But if I had to go back, I'd do it all the same all over again. I'd take every single minute I could have with her, even if it meant living all of these years not knowing what had happened."

"What did happen—do you know? It's not my business, but …?" I asked.

"I was away for a few weeks, and when I got back, Kay and Bill were gone—the apartment was empty of their things, and the landlord was showing the place to someone else. I went crazy trying to figure it out, but even though we knew so much about each other, I didn't know where to look for her—and I couldn't leave anyway. My wife was ... not well.

"If it was today, she'd probably go talk to the doctor and they'd figure out it was depression or anxiety or something like that, and they'd be able to help, at least a little, with medicine or something," he said. "But back then it was just—" he moved his hand around in the air, like casting a spell. "A mystery. They called it a nervous breakdown, and she went to stay at a hospital close to where her parents lived for most of that year. That's where I had been when Kay left. Visiting Sophia. She wasn't really *there*, most of that year, and Lord only knows what they were giving her. I thought it was the best thing to do at the time, but who knows. She came home eventually, but it just got worse. She'd stay weeks at a time in bed, and then one day she'd get up and spend a week cleaning the house all day and all night, like nothing was unusual at all. Sometimes she'd get paranoid about noises, even about me, and accuse me of things I hadn't done. When she was about thirty-five, it got really bad, and one day I came home and ... well you can guess, probably. I tried to be a good husband from the very start. But I also know I wasn't."

Bernie shook his head, and I could see the outline of his face as the sky continued to lighten.

"The time with Kay those few years was ... well, I lived on those memories a long time. They carried me through a lot of rough things. I'm not foolish enough to think that life would have been perfect with Kay, but I loved her very much, and she loved me back. We were equal, when we were together. We could take care of each other, and we needed that—not just to be taken care of, but to give it too. We're the same that way.

"Anyway, I tried to find her, but I didn't know where her family was, really—not enough to track them down, at any rate. These days you can google anything, but you couldn't do that then.

"Kay told me last week that Bill had come home one day with a telegram in hand from his family. His dad had died, there was no one to manage the farm, and his mother needed him to come home. So they did. The apartment was rented; it had been furnished, which was pretty common then. None of the stuff was theirs, so it was an easy thing to pack up and go. Kay couldn't think of how to leave a message for me, not knowing who else might see it. In the end, she wrote a note that said, 'We've had to go back to Bill's family farm. I hope we will see you both again soon.' She'd included an address, and then she'd slid it under my door."

"So—you knew she'd gone, then," I said.

"No. I never got the note. I did get an envelope with her gas bill and a cheque in it."

"I don't understand."

"She must have had both envelopes in her purse and mixed them up. A few days later, she stopped along the drive home to get a stamp and mail the gas bill, and then she discovered that what was in her hand was the note for me, instead. They were too far from home by then to turn around and do anything about it."

"So why didn't she mail you something later? She lived in the same building; she'd have known the address."

"Well, she did eventually. But with Kay gone and my job wrapping up soon anyway, there was no point in me staying there. I moved up to the town near the hospital. Kay got the letter back, marked 'return to sender.'"

I tried to imagine Kay standing in the farmhouse in PEI, with the returned letter in her hand. "Did she think you'd gone or that you'd sent the letter back in anger?" I asked.

"She wasn't sure. And she thought there was no point in trying again. So she just carried on, not knowing either way. And I had no clue she'd tried to leave me a message."

It made my stomach hurt to think of it. A series of unexpected changes and mistakes, and they'd spent forty years not knowing where the other one was.

"How come you didn't look for her when you could? I mean, eventually you could have just sat down at your computer and googled her."

"I thought about it many times. I guess I was scared—that I'd get up my hopes and then not find her. What if she was dead, or worse? It had been so long that I guess I got used to living without her and living with just the memory of her." He shook his head. "I can't imagine it now. That was just a few weeks ago, and already I can't imagine going back to that."

"No, I can't imagine it either," I said. "You guys work really well together."

He nodded. "So, that's how I know what I'm talking about, when I tell you that your story isn't done," he said, smiling at me. "You haven't even started yet, Ruthie."

He pointed out to the horizon, and I turned and followed his finger. There it was, the orange glow outlining the whole mountain range, the edge of the sun just peeking above the tip of the mountain. The light was golden and pink, and the air warmed suddenly by a couple of degrees. I shielded my eyes from it, not looking right at the sun but at the sky all around it: beautiful colours blending and shifting, an earthly aurora borealis in slow motion.

I thought of David and wished he was sitting here with me to see it. He'd love it, I was sure. He'd love the isolation and the quiet and the view and the simple pleasure of it all.

I loved the symbolism of it, the "new day has broken" feeling it gave me. Like anything was possible, like I might just get through the day without screwing anything up, like the sunrise was infusing me with a little bit of its power.

We sat in silence for another ten minutes, until the sun was fully over the edge of the range, and then Bernie opened the backpack and pulled out a brown paper bag. He'd brought muffins and bananas, and he handed me one of each.

"Breakfast on the mountaintop," he said.

"Best view I've ever had for a meal," I replied.

He smiled and nodded. We ate our food in silence, and as we wrapped up the garbage and put it back in the backpack, Bernie cleared his throat.

"Ruthie, you should go see David."

"Oh, I don't think he—"

"You don't know that. And you won't unless you try. And if you don't try, you'll always wonder."

"What if I showed up and he turned me away? I'm not sure I could handle that," I said.

"You could. I don't think it's very likely, but if it happened that way, you'd carry on. And at least you'd *know*."

"Maybe."

"Don't waste your years wondering."

I looked at him, at his lined face that always looked a little sad, even when he was laughing, marked by years of wondering.

"I think I've just messed up so many things already," I said. "I haven't done anything I was supposed to. Nothing has gone the way I thought it would. And then there's all of this," I said, spreading my hands out to indicate what "this" might mean: the secret emails, Kay's injury, the hospital, the last week of silence from David. "What if I do something that makes it worse?"

Even as the words came out of my mouth, I was thinking about how small my failures and losses were, compared to his, or to David's or Kay's. Compared to most people, really.

If Bernie thought it silly or petty, he didn't indicate it, but simply nodded in a way that felt empathetic. His presence was safe and solid next to me as the sky continued to lighten by degrees every few seconds.

"You ever heard of desire lines, Ruthie?"

I shook my head no.

"It's a term that city planners use. They spend all this time designing a park, let's say. A path should go here, and another one there, and so on. And then a year later there's all these little footpaths where the grass has been worn down, in between the real paths, criss-cross, where no one had thought the paths should go. Those are desire lines: where people want to go, even when there's a route laid out for them already."

I didn't say anything.

"You don't have to stay on the path, Ruthie. Maybe the path is for other people. Maybe the path is boring, even, and the route you need is somewhere in between. Your own desire line. You're already on it now, I think. Just keep going. And see."

It sounded so rational and simple when he put it that way. I could feel myself close to tears and sniffed my nose, to stop before I began. Had I managed to go a single day without crying this entire week?

He reached over and squeezed my shoulder, a gentleness I leaned into. "Just keep going. And see," he repeated.

Then he cleared his throat again, like a cap-end to the conversation. "Well, that's enough metaphors for one morning, I think," he said. "Shall we go tell Kay to check off the sunrise now?"

I nodded, grateful to busy myself with getting back down the mountain.

28

I PUT MY BAGS in the back of the van and closed the rear door, then returned to the driver's side, where Bernie and Kay were standing.

"I checked all the route information," said Bernie. "Roads are clear, and no snow predicted for today or tomorrow, so if you stay on schedule, you should be fine. There might be a little through Manning Park, but once you get through to Hope, you'll be fine the rest of the way in."

I knew exactly what he was referring to, having pored over the map two dozen times.

"Thank you, guys. For everything," I said. I hugged them both, and they told me to come back and visit soon. Kay had made me promise I'd call as soon as I got there, and to keep her "posted," which she clarified meant "tell me what my idiot son does."

It was hard to get in the van and leave—aside from the fact that I was enjoying the time I'd had with them, I'd never really gone anywhere in this vehicle without Kay. More to the point, it meant that whatever I was going to do would have to be decided by me, starting now. As soon as I pulled out of the driveway, I'd be in charge of my own plan. I waited for fear or hesitation, but there wasn't any.

I got into the car, started the engine, unrolled the window and waved to Kay and Bernie as I backed out onto the street.

"Bye! Bye! Bye!" I shouted over and over as though I might never see them again, which seemed both impossible and very likely, all things considered.

They waved back, and when I got out onto the road, I put the car in drive and pushed on the gas, waving one last time for good measure. I got to the stop sign at the corner, and a loud bang erupted from the engine. Within seconds, smoke was pouring out from the edges of the hood. I opened the door to get out as Bernie came running.

"I knew I heard something that didn't sound right," he muttered as he popped the hood release button. As he lifted the heavy cover and exposed the engine, a cloud of smoke mushroomed out, and he leaned back to let it clear—which was lucky, because a second later the engine caught fire, the flames leaping out with a noise like rushing wind.

I jumped out of the car and raced to the tailgate to pull out my suitcases. Bernie shouted that he was going for the fire extinguisher, and I pulled out my phone to call 911. By the time he returned with the red canister, the flames were licking around the raised hood; I took the extinguisher and doused the flames, letting Bernie catch his breath as Kay hobbled out to the end of the driveway on her crutches.

The front end of the vehicle was covered in white foam when the fire truck pulled in and the crew took over.

I refused to see it as a bad omen, but instead a test: How determined was I, really, to get to the coast, all by myself?

"Guess I'm going to need to look up the bus schedule," I said, trying for a grin. "Plan B. Or Plan C? Or whatever letter I'm on now. I've lost track."

And for the first time in a long time, maybe for the first time ever, I didn't care that I had no idea what would happen next. I'd figure it out, eventually—Plan B or C or X, Y, Z—and that was good enough.

❋

The Greyhound, it turned out, was both a better and worse way to travel than going by myself in the van. I didn't have to drive, watch out for traffic or wildlife, or stop for gas, which was all a bonus. But the route wasn't exactly direct or quick, and with a half-dozen stops along the way, it was almost twenty-four hours before we pulled into Pacific Central Station in downtown Vancouver, where the trains and buses coming from other parts of the country all dead-end together. I got my bags from the driver as he unloaded them from below the bus, and then I wandered out into the main station and found a bench to sit on for a moment while I decided what to do next.

It was an old building, vaulted ceilings and tiled floors with large columns, and I knew from the maps that if I went out the front doors and walked a few blocks, I'd be in Chinatown, then the downtown East Side, and then the business district beyond that. It was only a short cab ride to get to a hotel downtown, and it occurred to me that might be a good idea rather than to make a go of it on foot.

I looked at my watch: 9:03 a.m., Sunday. I was starving. I thought of Kay telling me about David and his habit of going for Sunday brunch at the same place every week, and I felt a desperate wish that I was there with him.

I could totally picture it. Coffee. Eggs Benny for me. What did she say he always ate? Pancakes and eggs? We could share a newspaper. Or talk. Or I could tell him a funny story about his mom. He'd like that.

I opened my phone and looked at the map. He had breakfast at this place on the main street in New Westminster, she'd said. He went by SkyTrain from his home in Vancouver, and he walked to it from the station, so it had to be close to one of the stations in New Westminster.

I zoomed out on the phone, following the blue SkyTrain line as it went from downtown Vancouver, past the bus station I was currently sitting in, through to Burnaby and then New Westminster. There were five stations there. Two were on Columbia Street. It had to be there. If he went every Sunday, then he was probably there right now.

I counted the stations between the bus depot and Columbia Street. Ten stops. I googled the SkyTrain line to see how long that would take. Less than thirty minutes.

I closed my eyes and took a deep breath. I felt nauseous. What were the chances he was even there? Or that I could find the one place he'd be? What if I showed up and he refused to speak to me?

"It's better to know, Ruthie," I said to myself in a whisper, echoing Bernie's words from our mountain visit. "Don't think about it, just go."

So I did. I grabbed my two suitcases, threw my purse over my shoulder and marched out the front of the building, looking around till I spotted the SkyTrain station a hundred metres away. It took a minute to walk there, another five to figure out how to get a ticket, and before I knew it I was on a train on the raised track, watching the rooftops of houses disappear under me. Even Quebec City had not seemed this large—an endless grid of houses and streets and more houses and more streets.

I looked at the map. At which stop should I get off? New Westminster station or Columbia Station? I still hadn't decided when I realized with a start that we were at Twenty-second Street, the first station in the city limits. It was now or never.

We pulled into New Westminster station, which was a raised platform built inside a business complex. The area was surrounded by shops: a movie theatre, a chocolate shop, a few restaurants. My gut instinct told me it wasn't here, so I let the doors open and close and stayed seated.

It was less than a minute to the next station, maybe less, and I hopped out, pulling my bags behind me, and figured out how to get to the exit and back to street level.

It had started to drizzle while I'd been on the train. I pulled up my hood and looked around. Across the way there was Greek restaurant, and next to me a 7-Eleven. All I could do was guess, so I turned right and started up the street, passing a police station, coffee shops and other small businesses along the way, eventually arriving at a row of bridal shops. I crossed the street and doubled back on the other side. I didn't notice the small restaurant till I was nearly past it, and I only realized it was there when someone opened the door and the bell jingled. The words Joan's Diner were painted across the small front window.

I slowed and looked through the window—right at David, who was eating pancakes and reading a newspaper, just as I'd imagined.

I was frozen to the spot, unable to move or say anything. David hadn't noticed me at all. He was engrossed in the paper, reading, his head tilted slightly to the side, away from me. If I waved, it might catch his attention, but I could also leave, and he'd be none the wiser.

I turned my back to the window and considered the options. I could walk away, get back on the SkyTrain downtown, check into a hotel, enjoy some sightseeing and then head back to PEI. My stomach sank just thinking of it. I probably didn't belong here in Vancouver, but I definitely didn't belong there either. Or in Shawville. Or in Rossland.

Instead of a surge of loneliness at the thought, I felt instead a sudden freedom. No one was waiting for me. No one assumed or expected anything. I didn't belong anywhere, or to anyone—except to myself.

The idea of David was compelling and magnetic, but was it real, or had it just been a convenient distraction these last weeks? No matter how David felt about me being here, the real test was mine: How did I feel about David?

My phone beeped in my pocket. *Saved by the bell*, I thought. Distraction, at least for a moment. I pulled it out and looked at the screen. It was Jules.

I'm sorry too. Can we just agree that we're both kind of jerks sometimes and keep being friends? Call me when you can. I want to hear how things are going with Mr. Hottie and his mom.

Jules, despite everything, wasn't gone from me forever; it made me giddy and lightheaded with relief. I started to type a response, then paused. What to tell her first?

I'm just about to meet David. Like, in a few seconds. Kind of terrified. It's a long story.

The response was immediate: *Lucky bastard, to have a chance at a girl like you.*

Maybe. Haven't decided yet, if he has a chance. Or vice versa. Might be hello, might be goodbye. Wish me luck.

Luck, xoxo

I grinned, put the phone in my pocket, took a deep breath and turned back around to the window. I started to raise my hand, to wave, but he looked up just then and froze, a bite of pancake on his fork halfway to his mouth, forgotten.

We stared at each other for a full five seconds, then ten. It seemed like forever, like longer than I'd been travelling across the country, longer than anything that came before it, and then it was over. He looked down at the table and shook his head, as if talking himself into—or maybe out of—something.

I waited, and I thought of Kay, telling me that I couldn't spend my life waiting for the other shoe to drop, looking for the thing that could go wrong and always finding it. I thought about Bernie, how he hadn't known what had happened or where Kay had gone, but still he had saved room for her.

If this place was not the right one for me—if I wasn't supposed to be here on a Sunday morning in this diner with David—then it just wasn't. And there was no way to know, without doing exactly what I was doing right now. I took a deep breath and imagined putting my feet in the ocean and all the other things I might do, or not do, after this moment. Whatever happened, I was miles from home, or whatever I'd thought home was, and I was different now than I was a month ago. Life was going to change, and maybe it would include David, and maybe it wouldn't.

I stood a few seconds longer, watching him stare down at his plate. His silence seemed as good an answer as anything else; I hitched my bag up on my shoulder, ready to go.

But then he looked up and smiled—a half smile, slow and hesitant. He held up his cup of coffee and raised his eyebrows. A question. An invitation.

I smiled back. Nodded. Coffee would be good, and the ocean could wait a little longer.

About the Author

Christina Myers is a former journalist, a freelance writer and editor, and a lifelong book nerd. She is the editor of the BC bestselling non-fiction collection *BIG: Stories About Life in Plus-Sized Bodies* (Caitlin Press, 2020) and her writing has appeared in anthologies, newspapers, magazines, and online. A fan of red lipstick and dresses with big skirts and deep pockets, she juggles parenthood and creative work from her home outside Vancouver, BC.